THE HANGING JUDGE

The Judge looked at the jury. "You heard both sides of the case. What's your verdict?"

The jury was unanimous. "Guilty!"

The Judge picked up the Bible and his bottle, stood up. His instructions were brief.

"Hang him!"

Don't miss these other Western-action titles featuring Lassiter, the leanest, toughest hombre you'll ever meet!

WOLVERINE	(TOWER 51225)
THE MAN FROM LORDSBURG	(TOWER 51296)
SIDEWINDER	(TOWER 51307)
THE BADLANDERS	(TOWER 51315)
FIVE GRAVES FOR LASSITER	(TOWER 51409)
BIG FOOT'S RANGE	(TOWER 51428)
BROTHER GUN	(TOWER 51540)
DOUBLE LASSITER:	(TOWER 51285)
THE MAN FROM TOMBSTONE	
GUNFIGHT AT RINGO JUNCTION	

We will send you a free catalog on request. Any titles not in your local book store can be purchased by mail. Send the price of the book plus 50¢ shipping charge to Tower Books, P.O. Box 270, Norwalk, Connecticut 06852.

Titles currently in print are available for industrial and sales promotion at reduced rates. Address inquiries to Tower Publications, Inc., Two Park Avenue, New York, New York 10016, Attention: Premium Sales Department.

Lassiter #23:

CATTLE BARON

Jack Slade

TOWER BOOKS **NEW YORK CITY**

A TOWER BOOK

Published by

Tower Publications, Inc.
Two Park Avenue
New York, N.Y. 10016

Copyright © MCMLXXVII by Tower Publications, Inc.

All rights reserved
Printed in the United States

CHAPTER ONE

Lassiter was in Bisbee when the letter concerning Jeffrey Bannock reached him. He had forgotten Bannock. He wasn't thinking of old acquaintances, although it was just after the New Year, 1887 now on the books.

Lassiter was sitting in a poker game in the Copper King Saloon. He had a hangover from a week of celebrating, he was all but busted, and he was in the process of losing what little money he had left.

The man across the table from him, a whiskered miner named Hardrock Jessup, was doing most of the winning. Him and his slant-eyed, weasel-fased pal, Gimpy Lewis. The others sitting in were town men; they were losing, same as Lassiter.

Lassiter squinted at the cards in his hand. There was a dull pain over his eyes. His tongue felt like a thick cotton swab. Celebrating the new year was losing its kick.

Three kings! Ordinarily, good enough to win nine times out of ten. He eyed Jessup. The man had a waiting smirk on his face.

Gimpy glanced at the miner before making his

decision. Jessup nodded slightly. Gimpy raised ten dollars.

The man sitting next to him tossed in his cards. "Too rich for me," he said. He finished his whiskey, got up and left.

The saloon was thick with smoke. Scantily-dressed girls circulated among the customers. There were other games going on, and a lot of drinking.

Just outside and across the street a preacher named Jonathan was shouting hellfire and sin and predicting the end of the world. His daughter, a big, buxom girl with two long golden braids down her back, stood on a soapbox in front of the big tent and inveigled the customers inside.

Lassiter eyed his cards, the money in the pot. Enough to get him south for the winter. Vera Cruz would be nice, Tampico would be better...

He took out his last ten spot, tossed it on the table:

"Call."

Gimpy frowned, looked at Jessup. One of the saloon girls came up, ran her fingers through Jessup's hair, wheedled: "Buy me a drink, feller...?"

Jessup said: "Later." He nodded to Gimpy. "Let's see what you have." He put his money into the pot.

Gimpy hesitated, spread his cards out on the table. "Two pair...deuces and eights..."

"Not enough," Lassiter said. Maybe his luck was turning. He laid his hand down, faces up. "Three big kings—"

Jessup grinned. "Nice try, Lassiter—but not quite good enough."

He laid his cards down, one by one. Three queens, two aces.

Lassiter scowled. Sonofabitch did it again.

"That cleans me," he growled. He started to get up. The girl nuzzling Jessup said: "Oooooh...another queen..." She bent down, picked a card off the floor. "Just dropped out of your sleeve."

Jessup shoved her away from him as Lassiter settled back in his chair.

Lassiter's voice was soft, deadly: "Another queen, Jessup?"

Jessup shoved the table into Lassiter as he stood up, went for his gun. The girl screamed.

Lassiter put two slugs into Jessup's big gut and one through his right eye. The miner was dead before he hit the floor.

The noise in the saloon quieted down. Gimpy cowered in his chair. The girl edged away from the body on the floor.

Someone said: "Get the marshal!"

Lassiter looked at him. The man edged back into the crowd.

The door opened. Three men came inside.

The man with the badge was slender, narrow-faced, blond. He looked like a boy; he was thirty. He had a gun thonged down on his right hip, and a smile pasted on his face. No one had ever seen Johnny Ringo without a smile.

The two men with him carried shotguns.

They looked the scene over, started walking toward Lassiter. It was plain enough what had happened. There was Lassiter with a gun in his hand, a dead man on the floor.

Ringo said: "At it again, Lassiter?"

Lassiter's voice was cold. "Caught the bastard cheating, Marshal...he went for his gun..."

Ringo eyed Gimpy, the girl...they didn't say anything. His smile broadened, grew more cold.

"I don't like trouble in my town," he said softly. "And killings bother me."

Lassiter shrugged. It was Ringo's town, all right. The marshal owned the Copper King Saloon, had interests in another, and ran most of the whorehouses. The man had a good thing going here.

"No trouble, Marshal," he said. "I'll just pick up my winnings and—"

Lassiter paused as the two men with Ringo cocked their shotguns.

"Sorry," said Ringo. His voice was casual. "Looks like I'll just have to confiscate that money until after the inquest." He shrugged. "Town ordinance, Lassiter."

Lassiter eyed him. He knew what would happen to the money. He backed up a step, his gun down by his side, said bleakly: "You can hold that inquest right here, Marshal. Jessup's dead. I killed him. There's two witnesses saw it." He turned his cold gaze on Gimpy and the girl. Both of them nodded, dry-lipped.

"Need anything else, Marshal?"

Ringo was quiet for a moment. He wasn't

afraid of Lassiter, not with two men holding cocked shotguns beside him. He ran his thumbnail across his freshly shaven chin, said: "How much did you lose?"

"A hundred dollars—give or take a few bucks."

Ringo grinned. "We'll compromise then. You take back your hundred, I'll confiscate the rest."

There was at least three hundred and fifty dollars on the table. Lassiter eyed the slim lawman. He could possibly get Ringo. He couldn't get all three.

Ringo's eyes narrowed. "Don't be a fool, Lassiter! There's an old dodger in my office—a Wells Fargo poster. A sizeable reward goes with it. Just so happens I don't like Wells Fargo. That's why I haven't bothered."

Lassiter said drily: "Good of you, Marshal."

"Take your money," Ringo said coldly. "Get out of Bisbee. You're trouble, Lassiter. I don't want you in my town!"

It was a challenge. Lassiter didn't like it. But he had been planning to leave anyway.

He holstered his gun, picked up four twenties and two tens from the pot on the table.

Ringo smiled. "No hard feelings, Lassiter." He turned to the watching bartender. "Give him anything he wants, Frank. On me."

He scooped up the rest of the money on the table, shoved it into his pocket. "I'll have someone come in for the body...."

He stopped by the blonde girl, whispered something in her ear. She looked at Lassiter, smiled.

The two men with Ringo backed out, shotguns held ready. Lassiter waited until they were gone before going to the bar. Frank poured him a drink. "You got off cheap," he murmured.

Lassiter gave him a cold look.

"I mean," Frank said hastily, "it could have been worse. Ringo doesn't usually back off, even a little."

Lassiter shrugged. A hundred dollars was better than nothing.

He downed his drink, slid his glass over for a refill. "How much do I owe you, Frank?"

Frank was pouring. "Owe me?"

"For the room."

Frank glanced toward the stairs. "Oh." He shook his head. "Nothing." He grinned. "You heard Ringo...anything you wanted...."

He put the bottle in front of Lassiter and went around the bar to direct proceedings. He had a couple of men haul Jessup's body into a back room. A swamper scattered sawdust over the blood stains.

That was when the clerk from the Bisbee post office came in. He was a tall, gangly kid with pimples. He said something to Frank, and Frank pointed to the bar.

Lassiter was studying the fat nude in the oil painting hanging over the bar, when the clerk sidled up beside him.

"You Lassiter?"

Lassiter glanced at him. "Why?"

The clerk licked his lips. "Got a letter for a man

named Lassiter. Special delivery." He held it up. "Got a lot of forwarding stamps on it. Went to El Paso first, then Tucson."

Lassiter said: "Yeah, I'm Lassiter."

The clerk hesitated, remembering postal regulations. "You have proof?"

Lassiter took out his Colt .44, cocked the hammer back. "This proof enough?"

The clerk gulped. "Sign here, please, Lassiter."

Lassiter signed. The clerk left the letter, hurried off. Lassiter glanced at the return address. H. C. Culpepper, Esq., from a place called Rimrock, up near Santa Fe.

Lassiter frowned. He didn't know anybody named Culpepper, and he had never been in Rimrock.

He picked up the whiskey bottle and headed for the stairs, reading the letter on the way:

"Dear Lassiter:
This is to inform you that Jeffrey Bannock has passed away and in his will has bequeathed to you all ownership in his cattle ranch, the Diamond Bar. Time is of the essence. You must appear here, in the county courthouse, by the 25th of January to claim your inheritance, otherwise the Diamond Bar will be sold at auction to satisfy creditors.

H.C. Culpepper,
Attorney at Law."

Lassiter paused on the landing, frowning. *Jeffrey Bannock!*

It took a few moments for the name to penetrate. A long-shanked, sad-faced man he had met briefly during a flush year in Denver. Bannock was turning forty and taking it badly. A one-time Wells Fargo stage driver, he had tried his hand at robbing the company and been caught. He was just out of jail when Lassiter met him. They knew each other. Lassiter had held up his stage before.

They had a few drinks together and Jeffrey had hit him for a loan. Five thousand dollars would do nicely.

Lassiter had asked him what he was going to do with the money.

Jeffrey had thought a moment, a strange glint in his eyes. "Gonna celebrate my birthday," he said. "I'm going back home to rob a bank, rape a woman, and kill a man."

Lassiter didn't take him seriously. He had loaned him the money. That was five years ago. He had lost track—until now.

He considered the contents. He could make Rimrock by the 25th. He didn't like the idea of going north in winter. But he was busted. The hundred dollars wouldn't take him to Tampico. He was faced with the choice of robbing a bank or holding up a stagecoach—or heading for Rimrock to claim Jeffrey's ranch. He grinned. Probably wasn't worth much. But what the hell, anything he'd get out of it would be gravy.

He went up to his room, crossed directly to the dresser. He didn't have much packing to do. He usually traveled light.

He was bending over a drawer when he saw something move in the fly-specked mirror. He whirled, his gun snicking up into his hand.

The girl sitting up in bed was nude. She shrank back against the headboard, shivering. "Jesus!" She ran her tongue across her lips. "Boy, are you jumpy?"

Lassiter scowled. "What in hell are you doing here?"

She was the big dumb blonde who had run her fingers through Jessup's hair.

She said: "Ringo sent me."

Lassiter put his Colt on the dresser. It was right considerate of the marshal, he thought.

The girl pouted. "You coming? It's cold in here."

Lassiter took off his pants. It was going to be a long cold ride to Rimrock.

CHAPTER TWO

The two riders came down the narrow trail that dipped steeply to the canyon floor and emerged onto a more traveled road that threaded through the high-walled canyon. Here the older man reined in, his quick glance reaching along the trail, probing up into the cold gray hills.

"We've got at least an hour on him, Kid," he grunted. He had a bony, grizzled face weathered by years of bad luck and bad food and his coat hung loosely from a spare, wiry frame. His eyes revealed a thinning patience as he glanced at his companion. "We can ease up now."

The Kid nodded indifferently. He was a slight, frail-looking youngster at least twenty years junior to the older man. Close-cropped straw hair and a mass of freckles spattering his narrow face made him look even more boyish. But his eyes were gray, old, and hard.

Despite the rawness in the air, the Kid wore only a threadbare brush jacket which did not hide the bone-handled Colt .45 jutting from a tied-down holster on his right hip.

The icy wind made a dismal sound in the darkening canyon. The older man sniffled and wiped his nose with the sleeve of his coat. He didn't feel well. His bones ached. He was irritable, and he wanted to get this job done with.

A half-mile down the road into the canyon, a low-roofed structure, most of it adobe, made a T against the trail. The corrals flanking the building were empty, but a smudge of smoke from a wood fire whipped back from the fieldstone chimney.

"We'll wait for him at the Jurado House," the older man decided. "He'll stop there. Everybody coming down this goddam trail does."

The Kid nodded. "No sense waiting out in the cold." His quick grin did nothing for his face. "My turn this time, Hank?"

He let his voice ride high, making it a query. The Kid kowtowed to no one, but he had a cool respect for this slouch-shouldered man who packed two guns. Hank Bester, who had ridden with the Oklahoma guerrillas under a different name, was not a man to be taken lightly. Not even by the Kid.

Hank gave him no answer. He was frowning, blowing on his gloved hands, trying to work warmth into his fingers. "Damn the Judge and his law," he growled. "If I had my way, we'd have moved in on the Diamond Bar a long time ago."

He jerked his chestnut mare into motion, the action putting a period to his statement. The Kid kneed his cayuse alongside his partner.

Five minutes later, they pulled up before the

trail house. Hank slid stiffly out of the saddle and stamped his feet on the frozen ground. He levelled his gaze across the empty saddle and studied the road that led back into the winter-frozen hills. As far as his eyes could reach, he saw no movement.

"Take the cayuses into the shed behind the north wing," he told the Kid. "I'll have the drinks ready when you join me."

He waited a moment by the door, a wiry, dour man with thinning brown hair and features shaped by a hundred violent encounters. *Damn the Judge,* he thought bitterly. *I'm getting too old for this kind of weather!*

But he knew why he had been chosen to ride with the Kid, and he knew there would be a bonus in it. Maybe big enough for him to settle down somewhere....

He opened the heavy oak door of the Jurado House and stepped quickly inside, closing it slowly behind him. He paused, leaning his weight against the door planking. He stood motionless, slouched like some sleepy, mangy cat, his gaze ranging across the dimly-lighted, untidy room that was bar and general store. The stillness annoyed him.

Hank knew that Fresco Smith had seen them. No one came down that canyon trail without Fresno seeing him.

He raised his voice: "Fresco, you got customers!"

Movement at the greasy drapes shrouding a doorway behind the bar caught his attention. A Mexican woman, well past the age of flirtation, shoved a stolid, oily face into the room. Dull black eyes surveyed him in stony silence. Then the face withdrew.

Hank scuffed up to the short bar, toed a spittoon out of his way. Fresco came through the drapes as Hank leaned an elbow on the counter. The halfbreed was a slovenly, slack-mouthed man with a five-day beard and small, suspicious brown eyes. He pulled a suspender over dirty long johns.

"Yeah," he greeted Hank. "Wasn't expectin' company this late in the day." He brought a bottle of whiskey onto the counter and reached behind him for glasses. He poured and slid the glass to Hank.

"How're things in Rimrock?"

Hank eyed the man with cold unfriendliness. "Hard as ever," he said curtly. It was his stock reply to the question, but he was feeling poorly today and in no mood for banter.

Fresco guffawed, to be sociable. He refilled Hank's glass. "Way I hear it," he smirked, "the Diamond Bar's due for a new owner, any day now."

The cold stare in Hank's eyes stopped him.

"You hear too much, Fresco," the gunman said. "Let it stick between your ears!"

Fresco licked his thick lips, his gaze going sullen. "Only makin' conversation," he muttered. He glanced up as the Kid came inside, kicking the door shut behind him. The youngster moved with an insolence that grated on Fresco. But the half breed kept his annoyance to himself. The Colt on the Kid's hip was a lot of gun for so frail-looking a man. but Fresco wasn't fooled. The Kid had killed his first man at fourteen.

Hank jerked his head sharply. "Come an' get it, Kid," he growled. He turned his attention back to Fresco. "We didn't drop in jest to drink your cheap likker," he added grimly. "You're due to have another customer in about an hour. We want a few words with him."

Fresco looked from Hank to the Kid, who was openly checking the loads in his Colt. Hank's meaning was plain.

"Look," Fresco complained, "I don't want a body layin' around here. Damn ground's froze stiff." He pointed off. "Why don't you fellers wait for him up there, around the bend?"

The Kid's voice cut in with soft bleakness. "It's cold out there, Fresco!"

Fresco scowled. "Damn it, I've got enough trouble with the law—"

"We'll take the body with us," Hank cut in coldly. He slid money onto the counter, picked up the whiskey bottle by the neck.

"Bring the glasses, Kid," he said. "We'll wait for him in Fresco's back room...."

CHAPTER THREE

A road runner came around a bend in the trail and stopped abruptly, one foot poised off the ground. Beadily it surveyed the horseman coming toward him, as if wanting to dispute his passage. Then, thinking better of it, it turned with a flirt of its tail and disappeared among the off-trail rocks.

Lassiter pulled up at the bend and leaned forward for a better look at the country ahead. The trail looped in a lazy "S" down the bare slope, and far down in the canyon, he saw the smoke from the Jurado House.

"Reckon we can both stand some food," he muttered, scratching at the base of the roan's left ear. Most of these roadside places had lousy food and worse liquor, but at least it would be warm inside.

The roan tossed his head and whinnied assent. The wind off the higher slopes pushed against Lassiter's back, the chill prying through his coat, reaching down inside his collar.

Damn, it was cold!

Lassiter had been riding since early morning

and the trail house in the canyon was the first sign of habitation he had run across. He settled in saddle and swung his attention to his back trail. He waited a long minute before the rider showed up, a tiny dot cresting the far hill.

"That hombre's sure persistent," Lassiter muttered. He slid his hand down to the cold stock of his Winchester, then thought better of it. Could be that someone had followed him out of Bisbee; then again, the rider might be no more than a stranger who wanted company on the trail.

Lassiter grinned coldly. He'd have a good look at him when the rider showed up at the canyon house below.

His roan danced sideways on the frozen, rutted road. Lassiter gave him his head. Coming down off the main slope, his glance picked up the narrow trail which joined it from the north. Fresh horse droppings at the junction told him that at least one rider had come this way ahead of him. His glance moved on ahead, picked out the iron-shod hoofprints of two riders on a soft spot in the road, and shifted his attention to the trail house.

Two men had ridden this way from the north less than an hour ago, but he could see no horses at the tierack. Lassiter absorbed this, but gave no outward indication he was aware of it as he pulled up by the steps of the Jurado House.

Fresco Smith was wiping a wet spot on his counter when Lassiter entered. The half breed stopped wiping and stared at Lassiter as he walked to the big pot-bellied stove and warmed his hands.

After a moment or two Lassiter loosened his coat and Fresco's glance dropped to the plain-handled guns thonged to Lassiter's thighs.

Jesus Christ! he thought. *Another gunslinger!*

After a few moments Lassiter walked to the bar. "Too raw a day to drink alone," he said to the bartender. "Join me?"

Fresco automatically set up two glasses on the plain wood bar. He eyed Lassiter with a sideward glance. Lassiter looked bigger close up than he had first appeared. Something about him tapped a warning inside Fresco's head, began to draw on old memories.

LASSITER!

Instinctively Fresco's glance shot to the curtained doorway. It was a mistake which he knew Hank and the Kid must have noticed, and the bank of Fresco's neck grew stiff. It wouldn't take much to set the Kid off. He had a hair-trigger temper that matched on the gun on his hip.

"Corn likker," he mumbled, pouring. "Best I have..." He raised his glass. "Cheers," he said, and tossed it down, coughing as the hundred-proof burned its way down. "Burns the aches and pain right outta a man," he added, when he regained his breathing.

Lassiter had caught Fresco's look toward the back room and knew what it meant. He kept his gaze level on the bartender. He had seen Fresco somewhere before, but Lassiter couldn't place him. He shrugged slightly. What the hell! He had run across a lot of men in his years.

He picked up the bottle, poured another shot for Fresco. "Go ahead," he said pleasantly. "I'm paying."

Fresco let this one lay. "One's enough for me," he said. Then, jerkily: "You headed south?"

Lassiter shrugged. "Should be. Never cared for this kind of weather..." He turned casually on his left elbow, lifting his glass to his lips and slid an equally casual glance to the greasy curtains. "I'm headed for Rimrock. Never been there," he added, turning back slightly to face Fresco. "Can I make it before night?"

Fresco licked dry lips. "Not less'n you fly," he muttered. He was thinking that Lassiter wouldn't make it at all...not in one piece, anyway. "'Bout twenty miles from here, and the trail's bad."

Lassiter was killing time, waiting for the rider on his back trail to show up. Should be due in any time now, he figured. He wondered if the men behind the greasy curtain were waiting for him or for the new rider.

Fresco was nervous. "You hiring out with Pitchfork or the Diamond Bar?"

A ghost of a smile touched Lassiter's lips. "Kinda lost the habit," he said, shaking his head. "Hiring out, I mean."

He was leaning back against the bar, his glance idling toward the dirty windows. It was starting to get dusk outside...it would be winter dark soon enough.

He saw the rider now, framed by the putty-cracked windows...hat pulled low over his face, a shapeless jacket collar pulled up against the raw wind. Not a big man, Lassiter speculated...he couldn't make out much more.

But the horse under the rider had good lines...a big chestnut, deep-chested, still with plenty of go in him.

The chestnut's hoofs rang on the frozen ground, announcing the new arrival. It seemed to be a signal. The greasy curtains parted as Lassiter's hand drifted toward his gunbelt.

Hank Bester came out of the back room, stumbling a little, a half-full whiskey bottle in his hands. He eyed the bartender, said thickly: "Damn it, Fresco, need more wood for that backroom stove—"

He was faking it, and it showed. Lassiter eased away from the bar as he heard the rider come up the steps. It could be a whipsaw.

He grabbed Hank, yanked him up close, showed the muzzle of his gun to Fresco, said thinly: "Come around the bar, hands where I can see them..."

Hank stiffened. "What the hell—" he began, then froze as Lassiter's muzzle rammed into the small of his back.

"Don't move," Lassiter said grimly. "Don't even whisper..."

Hank didn't move.

Lassiter's gaze bored into Fresco. The bartender sidled out from behind the bar, shooting a desperate glance toward the back room.

The front door opened. The newcomer stepped

inside, kicked the door shut behind him and instinctively turned toward the stove. He stopped abruptly as he saw Fresco coming around the bar with his hands half up.

Lassiter glimped a brown mustache under the shadowing hat, little more. Not anyone he knew. Still, he shoved Hank away from him as the stranger's hand dipped inside his coat.

The greasy curtain shielding Fresco's back room blasted outward as the Kid, reacting nervously, fired at Lassiter. Fresco was jerking back and stepped into the Kid's line of fire. He staggered and fell against the bar, groaning.

Lassiter pumped three fast shots into the curtains, jerked his muzzle around and caught Hank with a slug under the older man's grizzled chin. Bester's gun was in his hand. He fell backward, the gun going off, ripping a slug into the ceiling.

Lassiter eased back, his gun trained on the stranger. The man was standing by the closed door, a small-caliber gun in his hand, a puzzled, startled look in his face.

"You in?" Lassiter asked grimly.

The stranger stared at him for an uncertain moment, then realizing, shook his head violently.

"Drop that gun!"

The stranger let the .38 hit the boards...he kicked it away, toward Lassiter.

Lassiter picked it up, his glance on the greasy curtains, waiting for some movement. There was none. He tucked the stranger's gun under his belt, walked past Hank Bester, who was dead, glanced at Fresco who was still alive, and parted the greasy curtains. The Kid was lying on his back, a ghastly smile on his pinched face, his gun still clutched in his right hand.

Lassiter reached down, touched the pulse in the Kid's throat, found none, straightened. He walked slowly back toward the stranger standing by the door, paused, studied him. The man avoided his gaze.

"You've been following me since morning," Lassiter growled. "Why?"

The stranger licked full red lips. "Sorry," he muttered. "Didn't mean to. I was just—just headed this way, too."

Lassiter frowned. "Coincidence, eh?" He shoved his gun back into its holster, reached out and started to search the man.

The stranger pulled back, voice rising in falsetto alarm: "Hey!"

"Hold still!" Lassiter growled. His fingers were probing under the loose-fitting jacket...he stopped suddenly, his gaze narrowing.

The stranger jerked back. "Damn you!"

Lassiter stepped forward quickly, swept the man's hat from his head. A mass of honey-brown hair loosened, dropped down over the man's shoulders.

Lassiter grinned. "Well, I'll be damned..." The hair, the breasts he had felt under the coat; the face...they were those of a well-stacked woman. The moustache...?

He caught the stranger in a hard grip, reached

out, tugged at the moustache. It came away in his fingers.

It *was* a woman!

CHAPTER FOUR

The woman stepped back against the closed door and said coldly: "You didn't have to do that, Jim. I would have told you."

Lassiter ran this through his head for what it was worth. She acted like she knew him—had expected him. It was a good act. Her mouth was set tight, her gray-green eyes flashed fire. Lassiter judged she wasn't too much older than twenty-five.

"Told me what?" he asked levelly.

This disconcerted her. She had obviously expected another answer.

"You know," she dissembled. Her gaze slid past him to Fresco, beginning to pull himself to his feet at the far end of the bar.

Fresco's wife watched from the curtained doorway. She was built like a wine barrel, her face mahogany-colored, twin pigtails down her back. She was Mexican, eighty percent Indian...she could have been any age.

Fresco turned to her. "Gina..." He tried to walk to her, stumbled, went down.

The woman went to him, knelt by his side. She didn't touch him. She began to wail, a low, sad sing-song cry.

"Christ!" the woman by the door swore, turning to Lassiter. "They're all dead!"

"Two of them are," Lassiter said drily. "I think Fresco'll live." He grinned coldly. "I didn't shoot him."

"Who are you?"

"The name's Lassiter," he answered evenly. "What's yours?"

"Lassiter?" He saw a frown pucker her brow, but the name eluded her.

"Laura," she said. Then, eyeing him, surprised: "You're not Jim Brannigan, out of El Paso?"

If this was an act, she was good at it.

He shrugged. "Never have been anyone else," he answered.

She sighed, shook her hair loose, took off her jacket. Under the man's wool shirt her breasts showed round and firm. Her eyes met his with a direct coolness. She was a woman who knew the effect she had on men, and had learned how to handle it.

"Why the disguise?"

"I'm in a hurry," Laura said. "I didn't want to stop and play games." She warmed her backside at the stove. "This way, men don't bother me. Most men, anyway," she amended.

Fresco's wife was rocking back and forth over her husband.

Lassiter went to her, helped her to her feet.

"Get some bandages," he told her, "and a blanket to put under his head..."

The woman stared at him, black eyes earching Lassiter's face.

"He's not dead," Lassiter said. "But he will be, if we don't fix him up."

The woman went back into the back bedroom. Lassiter motioned to Laura. "Give me a hand with him."

He turned Fresco over on his back, pulled shirt and dirty underwear away from the bullet hole just below his collarbone.

Fresco groaned and looked up at Lassiter.

"Couldn't stop them," he said bitterly. "Hank Bester and the Kid. Came in, took over..."

"Tell me about it later," Lassiter cut him off. He turned as Gina came up with a blanket and bandages. He took the blanket, folded it several times, placed it under Fresco's head.

"Get a bottle of whiskey, a clean rag and sponge off that bullet hole," he told Laura. "Give him a shot of whiskey before you do it."

Laura eyed him rebelliously. "Let her do it," she snapped, pointing to Gina. "She's his wife—"

"You do it!" Lassiter said grimly. "I want you busy where I can see you...."

He waited until Laura returned with the bottle and was sponging off the bullet hole before walking to the pot-bellied stove. The whiskey burned. Fresco's cry of pain came from behind clenched teeth.

Lassiter found the poker in the wood box, removed the stove lid, thrust it into the fire.

Laura eyed him. "What's that for?"

Lassiter ignored her. He walked back to Fresco, slipped his leather belt free from around his waist, doubled it. "It's going to hurt," he said to Fresco.

Fresco nodded. Lassiter gave him the doubled belt to bite down on, went back to the stove, took out the poker. Its end glowed red-hot.

"Hold his arms," he told Laura.

She stared at him.

"Dammit, hold his arms!"

She knelt by Fresco's head, held his arms down, putting her weight on them.

Gina watched, impassive.

Lassiter said, "Think of a woman, Fresco...any woman..."

He touched the glowing poker to the bullet hole. Blood frothed, flesh crinkled. Fresco jerked, a ragged cry escaping between his teeth...his eyes rolled and he passed out.

Laura's face was pale as a newly washed sheet. Her stomach heaved...she turned her face away, controlling it. The odor of burned flesh was strong.

"All right, bandage him," Lassiter said.

Laura's eyes blazed. "That was the...the most barbaric, brutal..."

"It'll save his life," Lassiter said bluntly.

He waited until Laura had finished bandaging Fresco, then Lassiter eased the unconscious man up, carried him to the back room, past the Kid's body, to a bed. There was a stove going here, too...the kettle on the lid steaming, the moisture comining with the cold outside to frost over the small windowpanes.

He set Fresco down on the bed and covered him with the blanket Gina brought back.

"You alone here?"

The woman spoke little English, but she understood Lassiter.

"My sister...husband..." she pointed toward the window. "They live down the canyon..."

"Will they help you?"

The woman nodded.

"I'll take care of the other bodies," said Lassiter. It was the least he could do.

Laura was going out the front door when Lassiter came into the bigger room.

He said: "Hold it!"

She turned, pouting: "Just taking care of my horse. Can't leave him tied up in the cold..."

He went outside with her, untied his roan. They went into the barn, Lassiter shoving the door open, letting the woman go in ahead of him.

A pair of mules stared at them from a stall...Hank Bester's gray and the Kid's steeldust were tied up in a corner, saddles still on them. They had not expected to stay long, Lassiter thought, at the Jurado house.

Lassiter examined the brands. Both horses wore a pitchfork burned into their haunch. Not a brand Lassiter knew, but he remembered Fresco asking if he was going to Rimrock to join up with the Diamond Bar or Pitchfork.

The woman was taking off her saddle, setting it to one side. She picked up her carpet bag, which had been lashed to the saddle, and her bedroll, then turned to Lassiter.

"Getting dark," she said. "Looks like we'll have to spend the night here."

Lassiter looked her over. She was smiling, waiting. What the hell, he thought. It could be worse—a lot worse.

CHAPTER FIVE

Lassiter carried the bodies of Hank Bester and the Kid and laid them out in the barn. The ground was frozen solid and he was not about to sweat out two graves for men who had been sent out to ambush him. In due time they would be missed and whoever had hired them would come looking.

The girl had her bedroll set out by the stove when Lassiter came back carrying his. An oil lamp on the bar was turned low. It was dark outside.

She was combing her hair, brushing it with long, steady strokes. She glanced at him as he came in.

"No room back there," she said, indicating Fresco's back room. "Looks like we'll have to bed down here on the floor..."

Lassiter had slept in worse places and with far less pleasant company.

"Which way you headed?"

She smiled at him. "Rimrock."

He wasn't surprised. "So am I." He went to the back room. Fresco was the way he had left him, sleeping. His wife was gone.

He came back into the bar. "Gina's gone."

Laura was still brushing her hair. "Went down the canyon to get her sister. She'll be back."

Lassiter spread out his bedroll by the bar, walked to the front door, looked outside. Pitch black now, not a light showing anywhere, and cold.

He shut the door, turned to Laura.

"You know the way to Rimrock?"

She nodded. "Haven't been back in two years. Received word a few days ago my husband died, left me his ranch..."

Lassiter put his back against the bar, eyed her. This was getting interesting.

"Seems we've both fallen into luck," he observed drily. "I'm headed for Rimrock for the same reason."

She gave him a quizzical look. "You had a husband...?"

She was being funny, which annoyed Lassiter. "A friend," he growled. "Left me his place—the Diamond Bar."

He saw her eyes widen, a gasp flutter in her throat. Then, coldly: "That's a lie. *I* own the Diamond Bar!"

Lassiter let a cold grin twist his lips. "What?"

She gave him a hard look. "Jeffrey Bannock was my husband. We—we separated two years ago. I'm his wife, his lawful heir, and I can prove it!"

Lassiter shrugged. He was too tired to argue the

36

case with her. He figured she was lying anyway. Bannock must have been twice her age. Still, the old goat must have stored up a lot of juice in the pen.

"You don't believe me?"

"No," he said flatly. He went to the stove, put more wood into it.

She stared angrily at him. "How do I know *you're* not lying? Why would Bannock leave the ranch to you?"

"I loaned him five thousand dollars," Lassiter said. "Right after he got out of jail."

"Jail?" She frowned. "Jeffrey never told me..." She settled down, made a pillow from her extra blanket. "The ranch is mine," she said. "But I'll see that you get your money..."

Lassiter was looking at her backside as she knelt and smoothed out her blanket roll. Her buttocks were round and firm against her Levis.

She turned, caught his look. "Something bothering you?" she asked coolly.

"Yeah," he said. "Can't figure you with a moustache."

"I've toured with an acting troupe since I was fifteen," she said. "I still have my makeup kit. Played boys' roles at first, later as a man..."

Lassiter grinned. "You look better as a woman."

The heat was spreading out in the room. There was a more persistent heat in his loins.

He went behind the bar, checked Fresco's stock of liquor. He found a bottle of brandy, picked up two glasses, poured.

He handed one of the glasses to her.

"Cheers."

She sipped her brandy. Her eyes shone in the turned-down lamplight.

"I'll need help running the ranch," she said. She waited for some reactions from Lassiter, found none, and added: "All right, then, I'll make you a deal. A fifty-fifty split?"

Lassiter was watching the rise and fall of her breasts under her wool shirt. He said: "I'll think about it."

He finished his brandy. She was sitting up, watching him.

He rolled to her, pulled her down on him. She gasped, tried to struggle...but there was no heart in it.

"Lassiter," she whispered, "no..."

His mouth found hers as his hand slipped between the buttons of her shirt, tore at her bodice, found a firm ripe breast...

Her breath quickened. "Lassiter...no...that woman...her sister...they'll be back..."

"Nothing they haven't seen before," Lassiter growled. He slipped his pants off, reached up, unbuttoned hers, pulled them down past her hips. Just far enough.

Laura quit fighting him.

Dawn was trying to find its way through the dirty windows when Lassiter awakened. Lassiter rolled over, reached out to Laura. The floor boards next to his were bare, cold.

He sat up, ran his fingers through his hair...Laura was gone!

He cursed himself for being a fool, pulled on his boots, went outside. The cold morning struck through him, snapping him wide awake. He made a run into the barn, a gun in his hand.

He didn't need it.

Her horse was gone, and so was his roan!

The bodies of Hank and the Kid lay where he had left them. Their mounts were still saddled, tied up in a corner of the barn.

Lassiter went back into the bar, turned toward the back room. Gina and another woman, younger, more slender, were sitting by the bed. Fresco was still sleeping.

"The girl," Lassiter said grimly, "when did she leave?"

Gina looked at her sister. The younger one spoke better English.

"Last night, just before midnight. Right after I came here. She said she didn't want to disturb you..."

She hadn't. And Lassiter knew why. She wanted to beat him into Rimrock. Maybe there was something to her story...maybe she *had* married Jeffrey. Goddammit, Lassiter thought, he wasn't going to be cheated out of this spread. Not by a woman. Not by anyone.

She had left at night, but she knew the trail in. And she had a good six-hour start...

Lassiter made the best of it. He had Gina cook

him breakfast, paid her generously for it. Fresco was awake when he looked in on him.

"Thanks, Lassiter." His voice was weak but grateful.

Lassiter told him he had left the bodies in the barn. Fresco nodded. "I'll have my brother-in-law take care of them..."

Lassiter went out to the barn, eyed the two saddled animals, decided to take both with him. He led them out of the barn, tied them at the hitchrack, went back inside, topped a mug of black coffee with a generous slug of brandy.

It was going to be a long cold ride.

Fresco gave him some advice just before he left. "Man name of Dave Carradine runs a spread east of the Diamond Bar. Steer clear of him. And— watch out for the Judge..."

The names meant nothing to Lassiter. "Sure," he said. He asked about the trail to Rimrock.

"Pretty bad in places...snow, rock slides this time of the year. Keep heading northeast. Useta be markers on the trail, but gun-happy fools have shot hell out of them. Be a couple of forks in the road...just keep bearing left...no way you kin miss getting to Rimrock..."

Lassiter left a dollar on the bar, took a bottle of whiskey with him as he left. He swung up into the gray's saddle, gathered up the reins of the Kid's horse.

He figured he had somewhere around fifty dollars left out of the hundred he had started out with. But he owned a ranch up in the high country and he figured if someone wanted the spread that bad, maybe they'd be willing to pay him five thousand for it.

The cold wind was in Lassiter's face as he headed up the trail to Rimrock.

CHAPTER SIX

Rimrock sprawled at the base of Tejon Peak, a cattle town now, though it had started out as a mining camp. Santa Fe ran a spur line down from the north, skirting the Gila River and cutting across the high plains country some ten miles outside of town. There was a watering station at the junction and loading pens which attracted cattle from the surrounding ranches, feeding them north to beef-hungry markets.

Lassiter came through the high pass flanking the mountain and down into Rimrock with a pale sun setting behind him. He had shifted over to the Kid's steeldust, Hank's gray on a lead rope behind him.

Snow still dusted the high pass, a raw wind pushing at his back. But the sun was warming the land a bit and it felt good against his shoulders.

A few townspeople watched him ride into Rimrock. The town was sixty miles from the county seat with rough country in between. It survived pretty much on its own terms.

One of the men who watched Lassiter ride by

was Jeb Stewart, standing in the doorway of his print shop, publisher of the weekly *Tejon Gazette*. Jeb was fiftyish, but looked older. Temper and hard drinking had taken its toll. His hair was white, thinning.

He watched Lassiter with idle curiosity. A drifter, he thought sourly. Bait for the Judge. A small anger burned briefly. He had a hangover from an all-night poker session and too much bad liquor, and he had been thinking of stepping across the street for a mug of black coffee at Ellie's Lunchroom.

Lassiter gave him a glance as he rode by and Jeb's head cleared slightly. That hard face under the shadowing hat reminded him of someone.

Wells Fargo didn't come into Rimrock, but some of their wanted posters did.

Jeb went back inside, started to rummage through a bottom drawer in his battered desk.

The *Gazette* publisher was not the only Rimrock citizen who noticed Lassiter. On the corner of Tejon and Main street stood the Territorial Bar, the biggest and most influential of Rimrock's half-dozen watering holes.

A stocky individual in range clothes had just emerged from the place, stopping on the edge of the plankwalk where his cayuse was tied to pull up the collar of his sheepskin coat. Lassiter's passage held his attention. His gaze followed the newcomer down the street. Then, swearing softly, he turned and went back into the bar.

Some range hands were playing a game of pinochle at a table close to the pot-bellied stove. All eyes lifted to watch the stocky man run past them to a rear door marked: L.C. SPELLMAN, Private.

One of the pinochle players remarked drily: "Wonder what's got Lefty all fired up?"

"The Judge's errand boy," the man across the table sneered.

Lefty Watts heard neither of these remarks. He was in a hurry, and in his haste he nearly committed suicide.

He put his hand on the door knob and was stepping inside the Judge's office before he remembered the cardinal rule the Judge had laid down—*no one entered his office without knocking.*

The slight, black-tailored, scholarly-looking man standing in front of a glass-enclosed bookcase had his back to the door. Lefty had this brief glimpse of the Judge before he whirled. A puff of smoke, flame-centered, blossomed from the muzzle of an underarm holster gun.

Lefty gave a strangled cry and stumbled back against the wall, clutching a bullet-torn ear.

"You blundering idiot!" the Judge snarled, his voice trembling with rage. "Next time I'll put a quarter-ounce of lead through that thick skull of yours!"

Lefty wagged his head, fear momentarily clogging his tongue. The curious faces of the card players appeared beyond the open door. The Judge walked forward, slammed the door shut.

"I thought I told you to ride back to the ranch

and check if Hank and the Kid had come back," the Judge snapped.

Lefty managed to put words together. "Was going to—" He walked to the side table where the Judge kept a bottle and glasses. He started to reach out for the whiskey with a trembling hand, when he remembered and looked back.

The Judge nodded coldly.

Lefty poured himself a shot, downed it in one gulp. The whiskey loosened his tongue. "There's a stranger come into town," he said. "Hard-looking drifter..." He paused, watching the Judge's face.

The Judge frowned. "How much you figure him for?" It was an old game, a means of income. The Judge was the law in Rimrock and strangers were fair game.

"Mebbe more than most," Lefty mumbled. The Judge had an unpredictable temper, and Lefty wasn't sure how the man would take it.

Spellman scowled. "A drifter with money?"

Lefty shook his head. "I don't know about money, Judge. But he's riding the Kid's steeldust and leading Hank's gray mare..."

The Judge rocked forward on his toes, surprise lightening his slate-gray eyes.

"You sure?"

"I'd know the Kid's horse anywhere," Lefty said. "And he rode by close enough for me to spot the brands. Pitchfork burned into the hide of both cayuses."

L. C. Spellman, sometimes known as "Lost Cause" Spellman, but better known in Rimrock as the Judge, scowled. He was a medium-tall, extremely slender man of fifty, but he carried himself with a military erectness that gave people the impression of greater height. He had a pale, translucent skin that didn't burn or darken and the long, iron-gray sideburns and clipped military mustache gave him the air of judicial solemnity he wanted.

Spellman had come to Rimrock a few years back with a battered suitcase, a copy of Blackstone, an expensive cigar and an under-arm Smith & Wesson .38 pistol which he could use with deadly efficiency. Behind him were years of varied occupations, including two years of on-the-job training with Quantrell's Raiders. The law was not unfamiliar to him; he had studied it and broken it with periodic frequency since he had run away from a military school in Virginia.

He had little stability and less loyalty to anyone but the figure that looked back at him from a mirror; consequently he had never married. He had arrived in Rimrock with some money and bought out a small, down-at-the-heels spread which he renamed the Bar S. Ownership gave him a stake in the high valley and mock dignity to his role as self-styled arbiter of the law in Rimrock. A friend in the Governor's office had mailed him a letter on official stationary, confirming his appointment as Territorial judge, this without knowledge or sanction of the Governor or the Federal legal department. But the official-looking document sufficed to intimidate those who might have questioned his authority and attracted those who curried favors.

Spellman ran a few cows on his spread, but shipped none out on the Santa Fe line. Yet somehow the Judge managed to keep men on his payroll, and through legal chicanery and unpaid back taxes acquired the Territorial Bar in which he made his permanent headquarters and from which he dispensed his brand of justice.

Now he walked slowly to the side table, absorbing Lefty's information as he poured himself a drink.

"A stranger to Rimrock," he murmured, "riding the Kid's horse and leading Hank's gray. Hmmmm..." He turned to Lefty, a small smile turning up the corners of his mouth. "That's horse-stealing, wouldn't you say, Lefty?"

Lefty's eyes widened. "Yeah—sure is!"

The Judge jerked a thumb toward the door. "Get the marshal out of that goddam whorehouse and tell him I want that horse thief brought in here for trial!" He paused. "How many people out in the bar?"

"Seven, counting the bartender," Lefty responded eagerly.

"Enough for a jury," Spellman nodded. He went to the chair behind his desk, settled into it, cradling his drink against his chest.

"Tell the marshal that Court is now in session. And get the boys out there ready for a hanging!"

CHAPTER SEVEN

Lassiter spotted the sign he was looking for and swung in to the hitchrack in front of a two-story, flat-roofed building with a parapet. The building housed a barber shop and a saddle shop on the first floor, and the sign was nailed to the building wall next to an outside flight of stairs.

The sign read: H. C. Culpepper, Attorney at Law. A hand, painted black, pointed the way upstairs.

Lassiter dismounted, tied the steeldust and Hank's gray to the rail and went up the creaking stairs. They ended on a small landing. Another sign reading the same as the one below but minus the pointing hand was nailed to the door.

Lassiter knocked, waited a while, and tried the door. It was locked. He edged over to the far side of the landing and peered through the closed window.

He could see a rolltop desk cluttered with papers, a bookcase, a pot-bellied stove, and on the wall a framed lithograph of Abe Lincoln. Closer, pinned just above the desk, a full-page picture of a buxom, plump beauty torn from the Police Gazette smiled winningly.

H. C. Culpepper, however, was not in.

Lassiter went back down the stairs and into the barber shop. There was a man in the chair, a burly dog at his feet. The dog looked up at Lassiter, bristled, and growled warningly.

The barber was a woman, six feet tall, four feet wide and weighing around two hundred and twenty pounds. She was a widow who had taken over the shop when her husband died. No one ever gave her any trouble.

She looked at Lassiter. "Yeah?" Her voice was one octave below a bellow.

"I'm looking for Culpepper," said Lassiter.

She pointed toward the ceiling with a pair of scissors she was holding.

"He's not in."

The man in the chair stirred, growled. "Windy? Hell, you'll find him in the Four Aces, lecturing the natives on politics, the evils of gambling and fallen women." The man pointed. "Down the street two blocks..."

Lassiter nodded his thanks.

Windy? He didn't like the sound of that. The letter he had received had been written by a man who seemed to know what he was doing.

He stepped out of the barber shop and almost ran into the muzzle of a seven-inch barreled Peacemaker.

The man behind it wore a badge on his coat and a sneer on his battered face. He was about Lassiter's age, but his features appeared to have been shaped by gun butts and fists. He loomed a full head taller than Lassiter, outweighed him by fifty pounds, and he was mean, having been rousted from his favorite pastime, which was bedding Kitty's girls.

"Mister," he said unpleasantly, "you own them hosses?" He jerked his thumb toward the rail.

Lassiter looked him over carefully. "Hell, no," he said blandly. "Ran across them just outside of town, brought them in..."

The marshal looked confused. This was not the answer he had expected.

"Where?"

"Down the trail apiece," Lassiter replied. "Anything wrong, marshal?"

Marshal Buck Winters was not long on thinking. He was an ex-pug, his face attesting to an unrewarding career in that direction. He owed his job and his allegiance to Judge Spellman. He turned now and looked down the walk to the man who had fetched him.

Lefty, still holding a handkerchief to his torn ear, said: "That's the Kid's horse he rode in, Marshal. The other belongs to Hank Bester."

The Marshal turned back to Lassiter. "Yeah," he growled. "Where's the Kid? An' Hank?"

Lassiter shrugged. "Beats me, Marshal. Like I told you—"

Buck Winters batted Lassiter across the mouth with the back of his free hand. He had an arm like an oak beam. The swipe slammed Lassiter back against the barber shop wall, brought a trickle of blood from his mouth.

Temper flared in him, was doused by the appearance of a gun in Lefty's hand. The Marshal, Lassiter figured grimly, he could take. Maybe even Lefty. But the odds were long, and this was not the time to test them.

"Marshal," Lassiter said slowly, wiping the blood from his mouth, "I found these cayuses, like I told you—"

He saw the fist coming this time, tried to twist away...the blow caught him just behind the right ear, sent him sprawling, his head ringing. He tried to get up, but was jammed down flat on the plankwalk by a booted foot planted between his shoulder blades.

Lefty came over and took Lassiter's guns while he lay pinned down. There wasn't much he could do about it.

The marshal hauled him up to his feet, shoved Lassiter back against the barber shop wall. "Let's go!" he growled. He jerked a thumb down toward the Territorial Saloon a block away.

Lassiter went. His rage simmered with every step he took. Was this a way to treat a ranch owner—a potential cattle baron?

From his doorway, Jeb Stewart watched the small procession as it followed Lassiter and the marshal to the Territorial Bar.

Another mockery of justice, he thought bleakly, another victim for the Judge's sadistic humor. But curiosity drew him. If this stranger was the man on the old Wells Fargo poster he had dug up, the Judge might find himself with a tiger by the tail....

The Territorial Bar was cleared, chairs for the jury lined up against the north wall. All the tables save one had been hauled into a back room and stacked.

Spellman sat behind the one table facing the door; he was wearing his judicial robes, a long black coat, a black top hat. A Bible and a bottle of whiskey were on the table in front of him.

Seven men were already seated as a jury, the bartender, a long-faced, doleful man, still wearing his dirty apron. A few spectators started coming in, sidling up against the back wall to watch.

A few minutes later, Marshal Winters showed up, shoving Lassiter in ahead of him. Lefty came in behind them. He set Lassiter's guns on the table by the Bible, and stepped back behind the Marshal.

"Here's the hoss thief, Judge," the Marshal said. "Resisted arrest, so I had to calm him down some."

The Judge nodded. "You have the evidence?"

Lefty answered. "Tied up outside, Your Honor."

The Judge eyed Lassiter. "This is a court of law," he said solemnly. "You will get a fair trial." He leaned back in his chair, one eye narrowing. "How much money do you have on you?"

Lassiter shrugged. "About fifty dollars."

The Judge tapped a spot on the table with his

forefinger. "Put it down here."

Lassiter looked around the room. This whole thing was a mockery, and everyone knew it. He had run across a setup like this once before, in Texas—a scroungy old sonofabitch who called himself Judge Roy Bean.

He said grimly: "Why?"

"Court costs," the Judge answered.

The Marshal's cold hard muzzle nudged Lassiter behind his right ear. "You heard the Judge," the big man growled.

Lassiter dug into his pocket and tossed crumpled bills on the table. The Judge counted them, looked up. "You're shy three dollars," he said. He looked disappointed.

"All I have," Lassiter said grimly. He was getting tired of this. The man had his little joke and he was forty-seven dollars richer.

Lassiter turned to leave.

The marshal stuck the muzzle of his Colt under Lassiter's nose.

Behind him Spellman said: "You make another move like that and I'll have you hogtied." He waited until Lassiter stood facing him again, took a swig from the whiskey bottle, went on: "What name you traveling under?"

"Smith," Lassiter snarled. His guns were on the table in front of the Judge. Either the man was careless, or he was supremely confident.

"How do you plead?" the Judge said. "Guilty or not guilty?"

"Not guilty!" Lassiter snapped.

The Judge pushed the Bible toward Lassiter. "Put your hand on it," he said. "Do you swear to tell the truth, the whole truth, and nothing but the truth?"

Lassiter placed his palm on the Bible, the marshal's gun prodding him. "Yeah," he said thinly.

"Tell your story to the jury," the Judge said. He leaned back in his chair, stuck a cigar in his mouth, lighted up.

Lassiter looked at the seven men seated along the north wall. He was getting angry.

"I found those horses," he said.

"Where?" It was the Judge interrogating.

"At the Jurado House. I put up there for the night. I was riding a roan branded TJ. It was gone when I got up this morning."

"And you just happened to find those two horses in its place?"

Lassiter nodded. "That's about the size of it."

"That's a lie, your Honor," said Lefty. "Those are Pitchfork horses. The Kid an' Hank Bester were riding them yesterday. I say this drifter killed them, stole their horses."

The Judge looked at the jury. "You heard both sides of the case. What's your verdict?"

The jury was unanimous. "Guilty!"

The Judge picked up the Bible and his bottle, stood up. His instructions were brief.

"Hang him!"

He turned and started to walk back to his office.

Lassiter stared. The man was crazy!

The marshal put a hand on Lassiter's shoulder. The spectators were already filing out of the saloon.

"Let's go, Smith," the marshal growled.

Lassiter jammed his heel down on the big man's instep, whirled as the marshal jerked back, rammed his knee into the big man's groin.

Marshal Winters gasped, a choked cry of pain escaping him...he dropped his gun as his knees buckled, and clutched at his groin.

Lassiter grabbed one of his guns from the table, slammed it down across the marshal's head. Winters' battered face picked up splinters as it slammed down onto the rough floor boards.

Lefty was four steps away, turning, drawing his gun. Lassiter shot him twice before Lefty's fingers touched his gun butt.

He turned his muzzle on the Judge, frozen by his office door.

"Sorry, Judge," Lassiter said grimly, "but you've just had a mistrial!"

The Judge watched Lassiter, studying him.

Lassiter picked up his other gun, cocked it. "My money, Judge." He tapped the table with a muzzle.

Spellman walked to the table, tossed Lassiter's forty-seven dollars down on it.

"Your name isn't Smith," he said. There was a grudging admiration in his tone.

Lassiter shook his head. "The name's Lassiter." He grinned at the shock in the Judge's eyes. "I plan to be around here a while, Judge. I'm taking over at the Diamond Bar!"

The marshal was stirring. Lassiter planted his foot down between the man's shoulder blades, drove his face down into the floor boards again. He picked up the marshal's big Peacemaker, fired six rounds into the ceiling, tossed the empty gun across the room.

No one moved as Lassiter eased to the door. He stepped outside and turned as a big, paunchy man with mutton-chop whiskers and a bulbous, whiskey nose said: "Lassiter?"

Lassiter looked at him.

"I'm your attorney, H. C. Culpepper," the man said. "Let's go to my office and talk."

CHAPTER EIGHT

Culpepper put more wood in the stove, said: "You took your time getting here, Lassiter." He walked to a wall calendar, jabbed his finger at a date, said: "Left me just two days to file for you."

"Where?" Lassiter was standing by the front window, looking down on the street. The two horses he had ridden into Rimrock were tied up at the rail; he figured he'd need them for a while longer.

"County seat, sixty miles north of here," Culpepper said. He had a deep, sonorous voice that sounded good in a courtroom.

Lassiter glanced at him. "What about this Judge? The one who tried to hang me?"

"Spellman?" Culpepper snorted. "A phony. Penny-ante crook who preys on drifters, takes them for what money they have, jails them for a couple of days and runs them out of town."

"He wanted to hang me!"

"Hmmmm..." Culpepper tugged at his chin whiskers. "Don't understand why. He's never gone that far before..."

Lassiter shrugged. "What about the marshal?"

"He does what Spellman tells him," Culpepper said. He walked to his desk, rummaged around in a bottom drawer, said: "Thought I had a bottle in here somewhere..." He looked up at Lassiter. "You wouldn't have one around, would you?"

Lassiter remembered the bottle he had stowed away in the gray's saddlebag. He went down for it and came back. Culpepper already had two glasses ready. Lassiter poured.

"To the new owner of Diamond Bar," Culpepper said, raising his glass.

Lassiter drank to that.

"Jeffrey's will is legal, isn't it?" he asked. He was thinking of the girl who had claimed to be Bannock's wife.

Culpepper drew himself up to full height. "In every way. I drew it up myself. Jeffrey signed it in my presence. We even had two witnesses—Regina Tate, she's the barber downstairs, and a customer she was waiting on..."

"Then it'll hold up in court?"

"You have my word on it," Culpepper said. He poured himself a refill. "Mighty fine corn liquor you have here, Lassiter."

Lassiter's estimation of the man went down a couple of notches. Anyone who thought this rotgut was fine liquor either had no class, or was putting on an act.

"Jeffrey have a wife?" he asked.

Culpepper thought about it. "I never saw her."

"Did he?"

"Jeffrey mentioned a wife. Before my time, though. I think he told me she was dead..." He shrugged. "He was a strange man, Lassiter...kept to himself, and drank a lot, only came to town for supplies..."

It sounded like Jeffrey, Lassiter thought.

"What's the ranch worth?"

Culpepper ran his fingers through his side whiskers. "Not much."

"How much?" Lassiter scowled. "Five thousand dollars?"

Culpepper stared at him, began to laugh. "Five thous—" He walked to the bottle, poured himself another generous slug. "Place's gone to hell since Bannock died. Wasn't worth much even when he was alive. It's kind of stuck out there near the Breaks. Lot of drifters come through his place..."

Lassiter was disappointed. "Any hired hands?"

"Didn't need any." Culpepper eased his bulk down on his swivel desk chair and shook his head. "Jeffrey had a Chinese cook and handyman. Guess he's still there, if the Pitchfork boys haven't run him off."

Lassiter finished his drink. He had come here especting to get his money back, but it didn't look like he would now. What the hell, he thought bleakly. He'd sell for whatever he could get and drift south.

"How did Bannock die?"

Culpepper hesitated. "He was found face down in front of his place, the back of his head blown off."

Figured, Lassiter thought. Bannock wasn't the kind to die in bed.

"Know who killed him?"

Culpepper shook his head. "Sheriff from up-country took a look around, left. He doesn't bother much with Rimrock, anyway. Bannock didn't have any friends to speak of, and no one put pressure on the sheriff..."

Culpepper got up and hit the bottle again. "Like I said, a lot of drifters came through Bannock's place on the way south. Jeffrey had a habit of putting some of them up at his place." The paunchy attorney shrugged. "One of them must have backfired on Jeffrey."

Lassiter took his turn at the bottle, killing it. Culpepper eyed it, showing disappointment.

"A woman calling herself Jeffrey's wife beat me into Rimrock," Lassiter said, his voice casual. "Must have come through here early morning. She was riding a big chestnut, maybe leading a roan...?"

"Not this morning, she didn't," Culpepper said. "I was in my office early. And I assure you, Lassiter, no one comes through Rimrock without being noticed."

Lassiter dropped the empty whiskey bottle into Culpepper's wastebasket.

"How do I get to the Diamond Bar?"

"Ride north out of town, skirt the mountain, take the first wagon road east at the fork. You can't miss it."

Lassiter buttoned his coat, turned to leave.

Culpepper called him back. "I'll need proof when I file at the county courthouse, Lassiter..."

"Proof?"

Culpepper nodded. "Proof you're who you say you are."

Lassiter grinned. "Sure." He took Culpepper's letter from his coat pocket, handed it to the attorney. "This should do it."

Culpepper rubbed the tip of his nose. "Just proves you got this letter. Doesn't prove you're Lassiter."

Lassiter scowled. What the hell. He didn't have a birth certificate. He did have an Army discharge somewhere...

Culpepper was waiting.

Lassiter said: "Wait a minute. I think I've got something for you."

He went out, down to the steeldust nosing the rail, rummaged around inside his warbag, came back into the office with a folded Wells Fargo wanted poster.

Culpepper stared at it. "You mean...you want me to file this as evidence?"

Lassiter didn't know why not. Far as he knew, he wasn't wanted in this part of the country.

Culpepper swallowed. "It's your neck," he said. He pulled a briefcase out of its place behind a filing cabinet, dusted it off. "It'll cost you fifty dollars. My fee for filing."

Lassiter eyed him. He didn't have fifty dollars. "You'll have to take a lien on the ranch," he said. "You'll get the fifty and whatever charges you have as soon as I sell the Diamond Bar."

Culpepper looked disappointed.

"Train comes by the Junction tomorrow morning. I'll need some money for train fare. And a bottle of good corn liquor—"

Lassiter peeled off fifteen dollars, handed it to Culpepper.

"You want to sell?"

Lassiter nodded. "First good offer."

"I'll talk to Carradine when I get back," Culpepper said. "Dave owns the ranch next to the Diamond Bar. He's been wanting to buy the place since Jeffrey died."

"Do that," Lassiter said.

He went down the stairs, mounted the Kid's steeldust. No one bothered him as he rode to the first eating place he saw and went inside. It was run by a Swede and waited on by his daughter, whose breasts bulged as she bent over to serve Lassiter. He found the food good and appreciated the view. He left her a dollar tip and went outside.

A few people watched Lassiter ride out of town. One of them was Jeb Stewart. His head was clear, his eyes speculative. He motioned to his printer's devil to join him, and pointed to Lassiter on his way out of town.

"Take a good look, Angus. He's worth five thousand dollars to a man named Sidney Blood of Wells Fargo."

Angus was seventeen, gangly, freckle-faced. "You gonna claim it, Mr. Stewart?"

The Gazette publisher shook his head. "Not me.

But I wonder what the Judge will do when he finds out."

Lassiter was thinking along the same lines as he rode out of town. The Diamond Bar was eleven miles out of Rimrock, and the afternoon sun was sliding down behind Tejon mountain when he finally spotted the ranch.

It wasn't much of a place. Tucked away in a small valley flanked by rocky hills. There were no signs of cattle anywhere. But there was smoke coming out of the stone chimney of the ranchouse...

Lassiter rode up to the barbed wire fence stretched across the road. It was rusted, sagging, but the sign on the gate was readable: "DIAMOND BAR RANCH. Keep Out."

Jeffrey had never been very friendly, Lassiter remembered.

He dismounted, opened the gate, led the horses through. He closed the gate and remounted. He was halfway to the house when he spotted a puff of smoke in the doorway at the same time a bullet nicked his hat. The steeldust shied off. A split-second later the whipcrack of a rifle broke the silence.

Lassiter was out of the saddle and hugging the cold ground in a hurry.

"Hey!" he yelled. "What in hell are you doing?"

The voice that answered him was a woman's. "That sign means just what it says, Lassiter! Keep out—*and stay out!*"

Laura Bannock had taken over Diamond Bar.

CHAPTER NINE

Lassiter raised himself to one knee and yelled: "Hey, let's talk this thing over—"

The bullet missed him by six inches, caromed off a boulder, screamed skyward.

Laura was standing in the doorway now, a rifle raised to her shoulder. Inside the barn, or tied up near it, a dog barked angrily—a big animal, from the deep sound of it.

Lassiter checked his outrage. The distance was too far for a handgun, and she could stop him if he made a try for the rifle jutting out of the steeldust's saddle scabbard a dozen yards away.

Besides, he thought grimly, he didn't want to kill her. Not unless he had to.

He stood up, both hands high, yelled: "All right —I'm going!"

He walked back to the horses. They were cold, tired, hungry. The steeldust eyed him, nickered...it was anchored here, trailing reins caught between rocks.

Lassiter gathered up the reins, mounted, and rode back to the sagging barbed wire gate, opened it, rode outside.

The sun had gone down behind the mountain, the sky above it laced with fiery red banners. A chill wind came down from the north, reaching through Lassiter's coat, numbing his hands.

He rode slowly away from the ranch house, turning off the road, dipping down into a swale of land flanked by cold and inhospitable hills.

It was a long way back to town. A long, cold ride. And by this time a hornet-made town marshal and a cold-eyed self-styled judge would be waiting for him. He wasn't sure the whole thing was worth it.

He dismounted, picketed the steeldust, hunkered down to figure this one out. Anger simmered in him. He had been outwitted by a woman, and it didn't sit well with him.

Hank's gray whinnied, looked back toward the rocky slope flanking the swale. The steeldust blew noisily. Lassiter glanced at the ridge, his thoughts elsewhere.

Coyote, he thought. He saw nothing and turned his attention back to his options. Laura Bannock was alone in there, holed up, sitting warm and pretty. According to his attorney, Culpepper, Jeffrey had hired no ranchhands. Lassiter could understand why now. Didn't look like Jeffrey had ever run any cattle here. Wasn't enough graze around even for sheep. What in hell had Jeffrey been doing here?

Lassiter rolled himself a cigarette, his cold-numbed fingers spilling tobacco. If this was what

Jeffrey had bought with the five thousand he had loaned him, it was a waste of money.

But Laura Bannock wanted it. Why? There was nothing here for a woman...not even a living.

Lassiter watched the sky darken, the shadows start to creep down across the land. Soon as it got dark he was going in—

He finished his cigarette, ground the butt under his heel, turned as the steeldust snorted.

The voice from up the rocky slope said nasally: "That's the Kid's steeldust, ain't it, Joe?"

Lassiter froze. The voice was casual, but it carried the threat of a gun muzzle pointed his way...he knew the sound, and the kind of man behind it...he had encountered them before.

Another voice, flat and without emotion, said: "Yeah. Shore looks like it to me, Peters."

Then, as Lassiter turned slowly, Joe continued: "Goddam country's full of horse thieves..."

There were two of them, sitting saddle...they were halfway down the rocky slope, looking down at him. Ranchhands, from the looks of them.

One of them, tawny-moustached, had a rifle across his saddle. The other, sniffling with a cold, had his gloved hand on the butt of his holstered Colt.

They must have already been here, Lassiter thought—probably back among the rocks, waiting. Heard the shots from the ranchhouse, spotted him ride this way....

"Where'd you get those horses?" Peters asked. He was the shorter of the two, the man with the moustache.

Dammit, Lassiter reflected angrily, *these horses were getting him into a lot of trouble!*

"Yours?" he asked.

The mounted men exchanged glances. "Pitchfork cayuses," Peters said. "Same as ours." He brought the muzzle of his rifle up, levered a shell into place...

"Where'd you get 'em, mister?"

Lassiter figured the odds, knew he'd have to try to take them. They weren't going to let him talk his way out of this—

"Look," he said, setting himself, "I found these animals wandering around—"

The bullet hit him high up in the right shoulder, spinning him around. He went down to his hands and knees, pain shocking through him, momentarily blurring his vision.

The man behind him levered another shell into place and said wickedly: "Let's go over that again, feller. You found 'em *where?*"

Lassiter hauled himself erect. "Go to hell!" he gritted and jerked sidewise as the man fired again, the bullet slitting through his coat, burning a shallow gash across his waist.

"Real mean hombre, ain't he?" Peters sneered. "Joe, rope the sonofabitch! We'll drag him back to the ranchhouse an' hang him—"

The dog's low, ominous growl spun him around. It came from the rocks behind Peters, from the shadows thickening on the slope...and the move temporarily saved Peters' life.

The rifle bullet missed him by inches, slammed off a rock a foot to one side of Lassiter, whined angrily for a split second before ploughing into the slope...

Lassiter's left hand was jerking toward his gun as Peters turned. He killed him with one shot, blowing the side of the man's face off. The Pitchfork horse reared, throwing Peters. It backed off, trampling over the still figure, eyeing the big brindle-colored dog that slunk toward him.

The other Pitchfork man had his Colt out, but he was twisting in the saddle, looking back toward the rocks, fear drawing his mouth tight.

Lassiter shot him out of the saddle, then turned his gun muzzle on the dog coming toward him. The animal shied off as a voice said sharply: "Brutus...*no!*"

Lassiter recognized the voice, waited. Two shadowy figures came down the slope toward him. One of them was Laura. The other was a small man, an Oriental, black baggy pants, loose-fitting black coat, a pigtail down his back...

The pain in Lassiter's shoulder was spreading. He gritted his teeth, fighting the weakness in him.

"You hurt?" Laura asked. She had a rifle in her hands, but she looked frightened.

"Not much," Lassiter lied. He walked toward her, his gun muzzle trained on her middle. She didn't flinch, but the big dog, sitting on his haunches, growled ominously. The Chinaman coming up behind her stopped, slanted eyes watching, right hand tucked inside his voluminous sleeve.

"I heard shots," Laura said. "I knew you were in trouble..."

There was a blackness stealing through Lassiter. He nodded to the two bodies. "A little late," he said grimly. Then, through his teeth: "Who are they?"

"Pitchfork riders. Carradine's men. They tried to move in on me just before you came. I chased them out, I thought you were..."

She shivered in the icy wind. "Fifty-fifty?" she said. Her voice was small, conciliatory.

He shrugged. He knew what was behind her change of heart. She would need him if she wanted to hold on to the Diamond Bar.

He holstered his Colt, walked to the picketed steeldust, turned Hank's gray loose. It was an effort to pull himself up into the steeldust's saddle.

He turned to Laura, his gaze blurring. "Let's go home," he said. And that was the last thing he remembered as he slid out of saddle.

CHAPTER TEN

The sound of flames crackling nearby reached Lassiter as he regained consciousness. He smelled wood smoke, felt warmth enfolding him. Instinctively his hand slid down his side, reaching for his gun...finding none, he opened his eyes.

Laura was looking down at him, eyes anxious. "How do you feel?"

Lassiter took a moment to consider. "Good enough," he conceded. There was pain in his shoulder, but no throbbing. He had felt worse.

He sat up, worked his right arm. She had taken his boots off, and his coat. His eyes searched for, and found, his guns and cartridge belts hanging from a peg on the wall. The bandage around his side and shoulder was not professional, but it would do.

"I'm a lousy nurse," Laura said, "but I do learn fast." She held up a poker. "I used this..."

"Thanks," Lassiter said drily. She was tougher than she looked; he'd have to remember that.

He looked around. He had been lying on blankets spread out in front of a huge fireplace which dominated the room. The entire fireplace wall was of stone, hand cut and shaped and placed block upon block, old clay filled in around the crevices. A raised hearth extended into the one big room, and whatever cooking was done, was done here.

Off to Lassiter's right a small alcove with a heavy bright-colored Navajo blanket hanging in place of a door was probably the bedroom.

"How'd you get me here?"

Laura pointed to the small man standing by the window, watching them.

"Tuy Song helped."

Lassiter remembered Culpepper saying that Jeffrey had had a Chinese cook.

Laura smiled. "Tuy Song made some soup." She pointed to a pot on the trestle table. "You feel up to it?"

Lassiter shrugged. This was what he had inherited from Bannock...a hole-in-the-wall spread, a woman, and a Chinaman he wasn't sure he could trust.

It sure wasn't what he had expected.

He walked to the trestle table, took the cover off the pot, looked down at the soup. It didn't look like anything he had seen before, but it smelled good.

Tuy Song was waiting just beyond, hands tucked inside his voluminous sleeves, yellow face bland, almond eyes veiled.

"What's he doing here?" Lassiter growled.

"Belongs here," Laura said. She came up, ladled soup into a bowl for Lassiter.

"He was here, cooking for Jeffrey when I came to the Diamond Bar..." She looked at Tuy Sons. "Jeffrey told me Chinese worked the played-out mines around here years ago...there was a Chinese settlement up in the hills a few miles from here..."

Lassiter sat down at the table. "You joining me?"

Laura shook her head. "I've had supper..." Then, at Lassiter's steady look: "Oh, I'll eat with you..." She found a bowl in a wall cupboard, two spoons, and came back to sit across from Lassiter.

"You don't trust me?"

She had a beguiling look on her face, an innocence into which she slipped readily...her eyes were wide, hurt at the thought.

"No," Lassiter said bluntly. "Nor him, either." He looked toward Tuy Song. "He'll have to go."

"Where?"

"Hell, I don't know," Lassiter growled. "Wherever all his other countrymen have gone."

Laura stood up, eyes angry. "If he goes, I go!"

Lassiter shrugged. "Suits me."

She sat down, her anger fading as fast as it had come. "He hasn't any place to go," she said. "And besides, we need him." Her eyes fluttered. "I'm a rotten cook..."

Lassiter hadn't figured on her cooking.

"You ran me off the place," he said bluntly. "What made you change your mind? Why did you come out after me?"

Laura smiled sweetly. "My, my," she murmured, "you are a suspicious man—"

75

Lassiter reached across the table with his left hand, gripped her around the throat. Behind her Tuy Song took a step toward them, then stopped as Lassiter eyed him.

"Why?" Lassiter said grimly.

He eased his grip around her throat and she pulled back, swallowing, fear in her gaze.

"A woman's privilege," she said, massaging her throat. "You know how it is—"

"Like hell!" Lassiter growled. She had left him behind at the Jurado house, taking his roan, knowing he'd be forced to ride a Pitchfork horse into Rimrock. She had lived here before—she knew what would happen.

"I thought it over," she said. "I can't run this place alone..."

Her eyes followed him as Lassiter went to his guns hanging on the wall. They were dark and anxious. "I made a mistake," she went on, the strain showing now. "I shouldn't have run out on you at the Jurado house..."

Lassiter slipped a gun out of holster, hefted it in his right hand. Pain made its run down from his shoulder. Be a day or two, he thought, before he could use it the way he wanted.

He cocked the hammer, turned...Tuy Song, coming toward him, shrank back, eyes like wet black glass, reflecting fear...

Laura gasped.

"Lassiter, no!"

Tuy Song flattened against the wall by the fireplace.

Lassiter grinned, slipped the gun back into its holster.

Laura sank back on the bench by the table. "You...you shouldn't have done that," she said. "You've frightened him."

Lassiter eyed the small Chinaman. Frighten, hell! Not this yellow-skinned heathen!

He walked to the curtained-off bedroom, looked inside. There was a four-poster, solid walnut and out of place in this otherwise bare room, taking up most of the small area. A concession Jeffrey probably had made to his new bride...

A small window was hidden by bright curtains. There was a mirror on the wall above a small dresser. A lamp burned, showing off an old theater poster above a battered steamer trunk...

Lassiter looked back to Laura. "Where do you sleep?"

"In there," she said.

Lassiter grinned, nodded toward Song. "And him?"

She colored. "He sleeps in the barn."

Lassiter pointed to the door. "Get him out of here!"

Tuy Song was ahead of Lassiter. He padded forward, head bobbing. "Me go. No makee trouble..." He looked at Lassiter: "Solly," he hissed, "velly solly. No makee trouble..."

Lassiter took a step forward him and Tuy Song ducked quickly out the door.

Lassiter went to the door, barred it. Outside a dog barked.

77

Lassiter turned to Laura. "Your dog?"

She nodded. "Brutus. Raised him from a pup. Part mastiff, part..." She shrugged. "He'll let us know if anyone tries to sneak up on us..."

Lassiter walked to the bedroom. "Come on," he growled. "Let's go to bed."

Laura stiffened.

Lassiter grinned. "Take your pick. In here with me...or out in the barn with your Chinese friend."

Laura didn't move for a moment, then: "We're partners, aren't we?"

"Sure," Lassiter said. But only until Culpepper came back from the county seat and the ranch was legally his.

"Everything split fifty-fifty?"

"Let's go," he growled.

She hesitated. "You're hurt," she said. She ran the tip of her tongue across her lips. "You can't—"

He cut her off.

"Let's find out."

She shrugged, walked past him into the bedroom, and began to undress.

CHAPTER ELEVEN

Pitchfork sprawled along the Gila fourteen miles to the east of Diamond Bar, a large, legitimate ranch run by Dave Carradine.

Hank's gray followed the other two Pitchfork horses east, across the high plains country, away from the rocky ridges surrounding Diamond Bar, toward the Gila. A moon showed, crescent horns tilted in a cold, clear sky. They moved with a cold wind at their back, reins dragging, snagging on brush, holding them momentarily, pulling free eventually.

Coyotes followed them, waiting patiently, moving in once on Hank's gray, lagging a bit behind, only to turn back before flailing hoofs.

It was way past midnight when the horses came into Pitchfork's yard, pausing by the windmill-driven pump that spilled water into a large wooden trough. They merged into the shadows cast by a towering chestnut, began to drink.

One of the several ranch dogs came out of the barn to investigate...he began to bark, more out of curiosity than anger.

The barking brought one of the Pitchfork hands to the door of the bunkhouse to see what was going on. He had a rifle in his gnarled hands and he was thinking sourly of coyotes...they had been raiding the henhouse lately.

He saw the horses move under the tree, cocked his rifle, went to investigate...a glance told him all he wanted to know. He turned, ran to the door of the ranchhouse, began to pound on it.

A light showed against the window, then a young Taos Indian woman, twin pigtails down her back, young breasts pushing up against a flannel nightgown, opened the door.

The Pitchfork hand said brusquely: "Get Mr. Carradine! Something's happened!"

The door closed. The man waited in the yard, rolling a cigarette, cursing the pre-dawn cold. He was the Pitchfork wrangler, older than most of the other hands—deep-lined, weathered face, scraggly gray mustache. He had worked for Dave's father, a kinder, less driving man...he had stayed on when the son took over, returning from god only knew where.

He had known Dave Carradine the boy—he did not know the man.

Carradine opened the door, stepped out to join him. Dave was a tall man on the thin side—not yet thirty, eyes bright with some inner, unsatisfied hunger. His sallow face was long, hollow-cheeked, on the homely side. In a land and time when moustaches and whiskers were the order of the day, he was clean-shaven.

He saw the rifle in the wrangler's hands, said sharply: "Yeah, Wally? What's happened?"

Wally pointed toward the horse trough and started to walk toward it, Dave following.

The horses moved restlessly, their thirst slaked, hunger gnawing. Hank's gray whinnied tiredly.

"Came in a few minutes ago," said Wally. "That's Hank Bester's gray. He rode out yesterday morning with the Kid..." Wally ran his fingers along a bullet groove, freshly made, on Joe's saddle. "Looks like Joe an' Lou Peters ran into trouble at the Diamond Bar..."

Dave nodded. He had dressed in town clothes, complete to white shirt and string black tie...he looked more like a nighttime gambler than a ranch owner. Wally had never seen Dave dressed otherwise ever since his return to Pitchfork.

"Get the boys up," Dave said. His voice held a quiet reserve—a man with his emotions reined in, the turbulence inside showing only in the burning in his eyes. "We're riding to Diamond Bar!"

He turned, strode back to the house. Wally watched him go. After a while he led the horses into the barn, stripped them of saddles and blankets, turned them loose. There was hay in the bins, grain in the troughs...he figgered they had earned it.

He came outside, looked up at the stars. Be light in another couple of hours.

He let his gaze run northwest, toward Diamond Bar hidden in the distance. What was out there Dave Carradine wanted? Wanted badly?

It had never been much of a ranch...and it was less now. Jeffrey's folks had run a few cows there, years ago, some sheep...mostly they had prospected, picking over the dozen or more mine shafts in the hills bordering the ranch. Wally had never heard of them finding anything. They had lived dirt poor and they had died that way, old before their time.

But Dave Carradine wanted Diamond Bar badly enough to try to take it over by force, if he had to. He had wanted it from the day Jeffrey Bannock had come back...

Wally crossed the shadowy yard to the bunkhouse, stood a moment in the doorway to survey the sleeping men. He was going to be mighty unpopular in the next few moments.

He sighed, picked up the iron bar by the door, and began to bang on the triangle hanging outside.

CHAPTER TWELVE

The Pitchfork men came early, with the sun just poking up above the horizon...a half-dozen mounted, armed men, flanking Carradine.

The dog warned Lassiter, his growl prolonged, menacing. Lassiter was eating breakfast with Laura. Tuy Song shuffled to the window and looked out.

"Calladine..." he said. His voice was a sharp, sibilant warning.

The riders made no attempt to conceal their coming. Iron-shod hoofs rang sharply on the hard ground.

They rode up to the ranchhouse, pulled up, spreading out behind Carradine. Dave had a gunbelt buckled over his town coat, pearl-handled Smith & Wesson showing.

The dog held Dave's cayuse at bay, growling a warning. He was big enough to make Dave's big black stallion mince nervously.

Carradine eyed the closed door. "Call him off, Laura! Before we kill him!"

Lassiter stood up, pointed to his coat hanging

83

on the wall. "Help me put it on." His shoulder was stiff this morning, and he didn't want the bandages to show.

Laura helped him.

Lassiter picked up the Winchester propped by the fireplace, levered a shell into place. They went to the door, opened it...the early morning sun was slanting across the yard.

Laura said: "Brutus...go..." She pointed toward the sagging barn.

The big dog looked at her, clean white fangs showing, black tongue hanging...

"Go!"

He growled once more at the mounted riders, then backed off. He tolerated Tuy Song, kept a wary eye on Lassiter—but he obeyed only Laura. He had run half wild since Laura left, making his own kills in the stony hills behind the ranch.

Laura clapped her hands. He turned and loped off around the house.

Carradine studied Lassiter.

"You the horse thief they almost hung in Rimrock?"

Lassiter shrugged. "Wanted to. Judge had a change of heart."

Carradine put his gaze on Laura. "What happened to Joe Boggs and Lou Peters?"

Laura hid her fear. "They're out there, back of that ridge..." She wet her lips. "They tried to run me out..."

"I killed them," Lassiter said shortly.

Dave had expected it...he riveted his gaze on

Lassiter, noting the way his guns were hung, the look in Lassiter's eyes. No wandering ranch hand...not this cool, easy-smiling man.

"And Hank Bester and the Kid?"

Lassiter nodded.

"When?"

"Night before last. Down at the Jurado House."

Carradine's gaze flickered...he shot a look to his ramrod, a rangy, tight-mouthed man. "What in hell were they doing at the Jurado House?"

The ramrod shrugged.

"Waiting to kill me," Lassiter answered.

Carradine swung around to him. "I didn't send them," he said sharply. There was clear surprise in his voice.

"Somebody did."

Carradine dismissed the Kid and Hank, went to the heart of the matter. He leaned forward in saddle, said: "I understand you claim to be the new owner of Diamond Bar?"

"Co-owner," Laura put in. "We're partners."

Carradine's cold smile had a sneer in it. "I expected you'd be back. But I didn't expect him!" He ran his gaze over Lassiter again.

"Lassiter, eh? I heard that name somewhere..."

Lassiter waited.

"Why are you here?"

"I was a friend of Jeffrey's."

"Jeffrey didn't have any friends!" Carradine snarled. "Not around here..."

"You killed him?"

The question seemed to surprise Carradine for a moment, then: "Would have! Someone else beat me to it!" He turned his gaze back to Laura.

"I'm making you one last offer," he said. "Two thousand dollars cash for Diamond Bar. Take it!"

Laura shook her head.

Carradine looked at Lassiter. "You?"

"Not enough," said Lassiter.

Carradine swept his arm around in an encompassing arc. "Take a good look at this place, Lassiter! What do you have? A hole-in-the-wall spread, not fit even for a sheepherder!"

"Why do *you* want it?"

Carradine hesitated, a guardedness in his gaze. "Because Jeffrey Bannock owned it!"

He paused, leaned forward again. "Take the money, Lassiter! And get to hell out of here!" He burned a look at Laura. "And take her with you!"

Lassiter shook his head. "We're staying."

Carradine's rage showed briefly in his sallow face. "You fool! I could take this place right now—"

He stiffened as the muzzle of Lassiter's rifle came up.

"Your men could," Lassiter said grimly. "There's enough of them. But *you* wouldn't!"

Carradine saw death staring, felt fear brush him, pulled back. He was neither braver nor more cowardly than most men...he knew when to give ground.

He settled back in saddle, said: "I'll give you forty-eight hours to think it over. Then I'll be back! You'll either come to terms or we burn this eyesore down to the ground!"

He wheeled the big stallion around, then, making a sweeping motion with his hand as he did.

Lassiter and Laura watched them ride out, turn off down into the swale behind the rocky ridge. They'd be picking up the bodies of Joe and Peters...what the coyotes had left of them.

Lassiter took a look around the ranch after the Pitchfork men left. He found his roan in the barn alongside Laura's big chestnut. The Kid's steeldust was there, too, glad to be out of the cold. Laura and the Chink must have hauled him back to the ranch across the steeldust's saddle last night.

The barn needed repairing. The roof would leak in any kind of rain. An old spring wagon was rusting away in a corner. It didn't look like Jeffrey had done much ranching here...or much of anything.

What in hell *had* he done with Lassiter's five thousand dollars.

He found where Tuy Song slept, off in a corner of the barn, on old hay. A small teakwood chest held his personal belongings. Lassiter didn't pry. What the Chink had in there didn't concern him.

He heard one of the horses behind snort, and Lassiter spun around, right hand jerking stiffly toward his holstered gun.

Tuy Song stopped a few feet away, hands tucked inside his sleeves, dark eyes glittering.

"Velly solly," he breathed. "Not know you were

heah..."

Lassiter let his hand fall away from his gunbutt. *Like hell he didn't!*

"I sleep there," Tuy Song said, explaining. "Calladine velly mad. I come...ask Buddha...bling peace..."

Lassiter said: "Sure, go ahead, Song."

He let the small man sidle past him, walked to he barn door, looked back.

Tuy Song was kneeling in front of a small statue of Buddha on a shelf just above the teakwood chest, incense beginning to curl up in smoke from a small brass holder...

Laura met him coming out of the barn. She was looking for him.

Lassiter figured this was as good a time as any to ask her a few personal questions. They were partners, weren't they?

How long had she been married to Jeffrey.

She shrugged. "Two months. He was...an impossible man."

She walked back into the house with Lassiter. "He drank too much, smoked too much, seldom washed." She made a small gesture of distaste. "I don't know what sort of man he was when you knew him. But here...he was inconsiderate, dirty, suspicious of everyone. Lived like a recluse, wanted it that way..."

Lassiter's next question was obvious. Why had she married him?

Her face took on that look of sweet young innocence. "I was touring with a repertory company through here in an awful play called *Nellie's Children*. We were broke. And I was getting tired of one-night stands..." She paused, went on. "I met Jeffrey in Rimrock. I was hungry, didn't have a place to stay. He bought me dinner...he seemed charming enough at first, told me he owned a ranch, needed a wife..."

Lassiter didn't believe it. Not all of it. Still, stranded women had married strangers before.

She pouted. "Well, now you know my life's story. How about yours?"

"Too long," said Lassiter shortly. "And you wouldn't like it anyway."

He went into the bedroom, picked up his hat, checked the money he had left. Not enough.

He came back into the big room, picked up the rifle he had placed back by the fireplace, said: "How much money do you have?"

Laura stared at him.

"We've got a ranch to run," Lassiter said. "I'm going into town to buy some supplies. I'm getting tired of Chinese food..."

She went into the bedroom, came back with twenty dollars. "All I have..."

He took it.

She waited in the doorway while Lassiter went back inside the barn, saddled his roan, rode off. Tuy Song joined her, slanted eyes watching Lassiter leave.

Laura waited until Lassiter was out of sight before she said softly: "All right, you yellow sonofabitch! Where is it?"

Tuy Song's eyes didn't blink. "Missy Bannock..."

"Don't missy me!" Laura snapped. "And don't come on with that 'me velly solly' stuff either! I know you speak English a lot better than that. You and Jeffrey were pretty thick!"

She advanced on him as Song backed off. "I know why you've been hanging around here. *Where is it?*"

Tuy Song stood his ground now, his black eyes suddenly hard. "Yes," he said calmly. "I've been looking around. But I haven't found anything, Mrs. Bannock. Not yet."

Laura paused. "I guess you haven't," she admitted, "or you'd be miles away from here by now." Her tone hardened. "Dammit, it's got to be somewhere!"

The Chinaman nodded. "Somewhere." Then, pointing off: "Why did you bring that man Lassiter here?"

"He'd have come, anyway," she said. "And besides, we need somebody who can handle a gun, keep Carradine and his men off."

Tuy Song accepted this. "I think I know where it is," he said. "I've looked everywhere else." His eyes glittered. "Then Lassiter..."

He brought his right hand out in a swift, gliding motion from inside his sleeve...a scimitar knife blade glinted in the sunlight.

Laura shuddered. "Just make sure he's asleep," she muttered. "And make it quick—and clean!"

CHAPTER THIRTEEN

Lassiter rode into Rimrock with two calls to make before rounding up supplies and heading back. The few people on the street stared at him in surprise, but no one bothered him. Not a man who wore his guns tied down like this one.

The marshal was in his cubbyhole office nursing a headache, swollen testicles, and a battered face. He looked up as Lassiter came in, blinked, his jaw dropping. Then he heaved himself out of his chair like an angry bear about to charge.

The muzzle of Lassiter's gun stopped him.

The marshal's teeth grated. "You sneaky sonofabitch! What do you want?"

"Came to see how you were," Lassiter said.

"Get out of here, you bastard!"

Lassiter held up his hand. "A truce, marshal. I'm not looking for trouble."

Buck Winters stared. He was a slow-witted man, his emotions uncomplicated. He didn't like Lassiter, but he admired courage. "Hell," he growled, a grin spreading across his freshly-scarred face, "guess we came out about even, huh?"

"More or less," Lassiter conceded.

Winters pointed to his bottle of whiskey. "Snort?"

"Too early in the day for me," Lassiter declined. He put a foot on a chair, faced the marshal as the big man took a swig from the bottle.

"I straightened things out with Dave Carradine," he told Winters. "Gave him back his horses."

Winters' scar-ridged brows crinkled in surprise. "What about the Kid—an' Hank Bester?"

"Beats me," Lassiter said. He scratched his head under his hat. "What about them?"

Winters shrugged. Hell, if Carradine didn't care, why should he?

Lassiter shifted his foot from the chair. "Where can I find the Judge?"

"L. C.?" Winters frowned. "Find him at the Territorial Bar...no, wait...saw him drive out this morning. Might have gone to his ranch..."

This was a new one to Lassiter. He scratched his head. "Didn't figger him as a cattleman..."

"Owns a small spread upvalley. Bar S brand."

Lassiter looked disappointed. "Guess he won't be needing another spread then...?"

"Why?" the marshal asked.

"I'm looking for a buyer," Lassiter told him. "For Jeffrey Bannock's old spread, the Diamond Bar."

Winters took another pull at his bottle. "Heard you were the new owner. What are you asking?"

Lassiter lied a little. "I've got an offer of twenty-five hundred."

"For that hole-in-the-wall? Christ!" Winters stood up, towered over Lassiter. "Who's *that* crazy?"

"Carradine," Lassiter said.

The marshal shook his head like a bewildered dog. "Don't know why Dave would want it. Or anyone else, for that matter."

Lassiter turned to leave. Then, casually, as if just mildly curious: "Those two men you said owned those horses I brought in—the Kid and Hank Bester. Who they work for?"

"Carradine. At least, Dave pays them." Winters knuckled his lumpy chin. "Didn't seem to do much work for him, though. Saw them in town a lot, hanging out in the Territorial Bar."

Lassiter shrugged. "Reckon that's why the Judge was mad, eh?" He turned to the door. "Find me a buyer, Marshal, and I'll set you up in business. Any business you name."

Winters straddled his chair, winced at the sudden pain in his groin, stood up. He managed a grin. "A whorehouse?"

"Best cathouse in the Territory," Lassiter replied, unsmiling, "if that's what you want."

Winters sighed. "No chance, Lassiter. Take the twenty-five hundred. You're lucky to get that much."

Lassiter grinned. "If Carradine wants it, I figger it's worth more. Keep looking, Marshal. You'd look good in a cathouse."

The marshal came to the doorway after Lassiter left.

Lassiter? The name rang a bell. He went back to his desk, started to go through old dodgers....

Lassiter rode down the street to the general store, went inside, bought a gunny sack full of groceries and staples, a slab of bacon, some beans, and a ham. Didn't leave him much money left, but he figured to get his meat on the hoof. Carradine's range beef shouldn't be hard to find...

He slung the sack from his saddle, crossed the street to the Four Aces Bar, bought a bottle of whiskey. Ought to hold him for a while. Laura was not much of a whiskey drinker, but he didn't know about Tuy Song.

He tucked the bottle inside his saddle bag, stood a moment, thinking. Culpepper wouldn't be back until tomorrow. There were some things he wanted to ask the old windbag. Like why would Carradine want to buy Diamond Bar? He didn't need it.

And the two men who had been sent out to ambush him at the Jurado House...who had sent them? Carradine? He had a feeling the Pitchfork owner had been really surprised about the Kid and Hank Bester being there. If not Carradine, who?

The Judge? Why would the Judge, who had never seen him before, want him killed?

Lassiter swung up into saddle, headed back down the street. He rode by a squat, weathered stone structure with TERRITORIAL MINERS

BANK in gilt letters still visible above the door. The windows were boarded up. The bank looked as if it had been closed for a long time.

The thumping of a flatbed press across the street caught his attention...Lassiter's glance picked up the sign painted across the window: THE TEJON GAZETTE, and swung the roan in toward the walk. A town newspaper should be a good place to learn something.

Jeb Stewart was working the press when Lassiter stepped inside. Angus was checking the sheets as they came off the press. In back of the room, a middle-aged woman wearing steel-rimmed glasses was going over advertising rates with a customer.

Angus stopped as he saw Lassiter, his face paling. Jeb turned.

Lassiter walked up to Stewart. "Howdy. You got a minute?"

"No," Jeb growled. "But I'll take one." He wiped his ink-smeared hands on a cloth, said: "Keep her running, Angus." He motioned Lassiter toward his office. "Back there."

Lassiter followed him inside.

Jeb settled into an oak chair behind a desk. "I'm Jeb Stewart. Name's spelled wrong on the window." He waved to a chair. "Been expecting you."

Lassiter refused the chair, let his cold gaze hold the white-haired man.

Jeb reached inside a drawer, took out a Wells Fargo poster, tossed it on the desk.

"Didn't know Wells Fargo was looking for me

out here," Lassiter said. He came up to the desk, looked down on Jeb. "You making a try for the money?"

Jeb's grin was crooked. "Blood money never interested me, Lassiter. And I don't like Wells Fargo. But I don't care much for men like you, either..."

"Kind of leaves you straddling the fence on humanity," Lassiter said.

"Maybe. Seen too much bad to expect a lot of good in folks." Jeb settled back in his chair, his shrewd eyes judging Lassiter. "But until this country settles down, I guess you're a necessary evil."

"You kill the Kid and Hank Bester?"

Lassiter's eyes went bleak. "Why?"

"Hell, I don't care," Jeb said. "Good riddance. Now if you had only killed Spellman yesterday—"

"The Judge?"

"Judge, hell!" Jeb stood up, walked to the window and looked across the street. "Some day, I keep telling myself, I'm going to take the train to the capitol, talk to the Governor..." He turned from the window. "If I make it that far..."

"Who'll stop you?"

Jeb shrugged. "I'm the only threat Spellman has in town. He knows I know his judicial appointment is a fake, not worth the paper it's written on. Came in here one day and told me. Run my paper, keep my mouth shut, and I stay alive..."

He paused, ear cocked toward the print shop. The press had stopped.

He went to the door, looked out. "What happened, Angus?"

Angus looked up, sweating. "Jammed. I'll fix it, Mr. Stewart."

Jeb closed the door, turned. "Used to be a time I'd let no man tell me how to run my paper, what not to say..." He walked back to his desk, sat down, took a pipe from a holder, tamped tobacco down, lighted it.

"What do you want to know, Lassiter?"

"Jeffrey Bannock?"

"Strange man," Jeb said. "Folks settled here before I came. This was a mining town then. Iowans, dirt poor. Settled here, tried to make a go of ranching...had a few milk cows, ran some sheep. Jeffrey was a young man then, restless, I guess. Got into some trouble with a woman, wife of one of the bank clerks here..."

Lassiter frowned. "That bank across the street?"

Jeb nodded. "Was open then, doing a good business. Jeffrey disappeared right after...heard later he was working for Wells Fargo, got into trouble with them, too..."

Lassiter nodded. "Trouble kinda followed Jeffrey around..." He went to the window, looked at the bank across the street.

"What closed it?"

"Embezzlement. A hundred and fifty thousand dollars worth. Broke the bank, ruined a lot of people around here. Happened just before Jeffrey came back, paid back taxes on the old homestead, settled down..."

Something stirred inside Lassiter's head, nudging at his memory.

"They catch the crook?"

"Crook? Oh, you mean the embezzler. Yeah, they did. He was already dead. Found him on the floor in the bank. Heart attack, Doc Stevens said. Could have been. No bullet holes in him, no marks on him. Had a gun in his hand, though— German pistol he kept in a cash drawer. Never got to fire it. The sheriff figured he was going to commit suicide, but that his heart gave out first..."

Stewart sucked on his pipe for a long moment. "Guess he didn't want to live, anyway. Day before, his wife was killed. In her bedroom. She had been raped first..."

"What happened to the money?"

"No one knows. Auditors went over the books...entries showed the bank clerk had been mailing money to some address back East. They checked it out, even had the Pinkertons in on it. The addresses were faked..."

Jeb got up, went to the door again. Angus was still sweating over the machinery.

"Goddammit," Jeb growled. "Guess I'll have to go out there, Lassiter, see what's holding things up. The kid's good on typesetting, but hell on machinery."

Lassiter said: "Sure, go ahead..."

Jeb paused just outside, looked back to Lassiter.

"How did Jeffrey get to leave that rundown spread to you?"

"I loaned him five thousand dollars," Lassiter said. "He promised to pay me back one day."

Jeb shook his head. "You'll never get that kind of money back...not from the Diamond Bar."

Lassiter shrugged. "Heard Jeffrey got married?"

"Yeah. Didn't last long, though. She was young enough to be his daughter..."

Lassiter stepped outside. The cold wind hitting him reminded him he was a long way from Tampico.

Two men were waiting on the walk beside his picketed horse.

The older one with a cast in his right eye said quickly: "No trouble, Lassiter." He motioned toward the Territorial Bar. "The Judge wants to have a talk with you."

Lassiter eyed the two men. "I've already had a talk with him." He walked to the roan, started to untie him...

"He wants to buy the Diamond Bar," the man said.

Lassiter paused.

"Cash on the line," the man added.

Lassiter glanced down the street toward the Territorial Bar. What did he have to lose?

CHAPTER FOURTEEN

The Judge was in his office seated behind his desk when Lassiter came inside. The two men who had escorted him here stepped back and closed the door, leaving them alone.

Spellman pointed to three small stacks of bills laid out in front of him.

"Five thousand dollars," he said. "Count it."

Lassiter stood looking down on him, wondering what the catch was. He could see the money—fifty dollar bills on top of each stack....

"I'll take your word for it," Lassiter said.

The Judge took a paper from his desk, pushed it toward Lassiter. "Bill of sale. A legal contract giving me ownership of Diamond Bar. Sign it, pick up the money, and get out of Rimrock!"

It was tempting. The warm sun of Tampico beckoned...a dark-haired girl named Margarita...

Spellman reached into a box, took out a cigar, lighted it...he was watching Lassiter's face, a cold, thin smile on his lips.

"It's what Bannock owed you, isn't it?" he said. "You came out even."

Lassiter frowned. How did this self-styled judge know what Jeffrey owed him?

"Take the money," said Spellman. It sounded like an order. "I'm making this offer to you only once!"

It was the wrong thing to say the way Spellman said it.

Lassiter leaned over the desk. "And then what?" His voice had an edge to it.

Spellman met Lassiter's gaze, blew smoke at him. "I drove out to the Junction this morning, sent a wire to Wells Fargo headquarters. Specifically to an agent name of Sidney Blood. You know him, don't you, Lassiter?"

Lassiter nodded. "Bosom friends."

He leaned across the desk and backhanded the Judge across the mouth. The move caught Spellman by surprise. The blow knocked him backward, out of his chair, the mashed cigar spread across his bewildered face.

Lassiter stepped to the wall as the door opened. The two men who had escorted him here came inside and pulled up short as they saw the gun in Lassiter's hand.

The Judge got slowly to his feet, spat out flecks of tobacco. His eyes burned into Lassiter.

"You goddam fool!" he said, anger choking him. "It was a fair offer. You should have taken the money while you still had time..."

"Not enough," Lassiter said.

"How much do you want for that rundown spread?"

"One hundred and fifty thousand dollars," Lassiter answered coolly. "Not a cent less."

The Judge's eyes flared, went dead. He picked up the money, stuffed the bills into a large envelope, slid it inside his desk.

"Sidney Blood will be here in a couple of days." Spellman's voice was bleak, under control. "Stick around, Lassiter. I want to see you hang!"

He motioned to the two waiting men.

"Let him go!"

Lassiter grinned as he went out.

Laura was waiting for him when Lassiter got back. Tuy Song took the gunny sack, went to the sink and started peeling potatoes.

Lassiter had done some thinking on his way back. He settled himself in one of the two chairs in the room, said: "How much money do you have, Laura?"

She looked concerned. "I gave you all I had."

He frowned. "Not enough." He was thinking he didn't have much time left here. Carradine and his men he could have handled. But Sidney Blood was another matter.

"We'll need a couple of thousand," he said. He was thinking of Tampico again.

Laura stiffened, her voice icy: "You thinking of selling to Carradine?"

"I've had a better offer," Lassiter said.

She came and knelt at his side, her eyes softening. "Lassiter—you wouldn't sell me out, would you? Not after last night...?"

"Five thousand dollars is a lot of money," Lassiter said. He was looking at Laura, but out of the corners of his eyes he saw Tuy Song pause, saw the small tremor that went through the man.

Laura straightened, turned away, her voice cold: "I don't believe you! Who would offer that kind of money for this place?"

"The Judge did. Just now."

Laura bit her lip. "That old fake! He doesn't have that kind of money—"

"He owns a ranch—"

"A hole-in-the-wall, just like this..." Laura paused.

"I saw the money," Lassiter said. He went to the stove, poured himself some coffee. He looked at Tuy Song. "You're going to need more wood, if you plan on cooking supper tonight, Song."

The Chinaman nodded obsequiously. He laid the peeling knife aside, wiped his wet hands on a towel, went outside.

Lassiter turned back to Laura. "What do we need him for?"

"I told you," Laura snapped. "He cooks, cleans up, chops wood and—"

"And?" Lassiter said, a smile on his lips.

She flushed. "You've got a rotten mind, Lassiter!"

"You haven't answered me."

"Jeffrey hired him. Tuy Song's been a fixture here since I came. It's the only house he knows..."

She came up to him again, eyes searching, warm: "Don't sell, Lassiter. We're good together.

We can make a go of this ranch."

Lassiter's voice was dry: "With what?"

"We'll manage." Then, apprehensively: "You didn't sell to him?"

Lassiter sipped his coffee. "Why would he want this place?"

She shrugged. "How do I know?"

"It isn't worth what Carradine wants to pay for it," Lassiter went on. "Why did Jeffrey come back here? Why did he stay?"

"I have no idea."

"You lived with him."

She moved away from him. "I told you...he was a secretive man..."

"Why do *you* want it?"

She faced him, eyes bitter. "I told you. I'm like Tuy Song. I've got no place else to go."

Lassiter didn't believe her. She had met Jeffrey, married him. She could do it again, somewhere else.

Tuy Song came in with an armful of wood.

Lassiter picked up his hat and headed for the door.

Laura said anxiously: "Where are you going?"

"Take a look around, before it gets dark," he said. "I want to see why anyone would want to pay five thousand dollars for this spread..."

Tuy Song dropped the wood into the wood box as Lassiter left. He straightened, looked at Laura.

She nodded, her mouth tight, her eyes cold.

CHAPTER FIFTEEN

There wasn't much here that was worth anything, Lassiter thought. He pulled himself up into the saddle, his right shoulder feeling stiff again. Damn cold was getting to him.

He looked around. The ranchhouse was backed up against a sheer cliff, part of a ridge that extended from the mountain range to the north. Besides the sagging barn there was an outhouse, padded with paper to keep the wind out. It had a tin corrugated roof. Must sound like hell during a rain, Lassiter thought.

There was a spring about a hundred yards from the house, a well-worn path leading to it. Water enough for people living here. Not enough for cattle.

He rode east with the low sun at his back. Came across a patch of ground that had once been used for farming, a long time ago. Someone had spent back-breaking days hauling rocks out of the stony ground, building stone perimeters around the sterile plot.

Jeffrey's folks?

The answer lay just beyond. Two graves overlooking the farm area, wooden headboards down, the lettering on them faded, unreadable.

Lassiter rode past the graves, following scraps of barbed wire, rusted, stretched between old cedar poles which had rotted through the years, fallen. They marked the boundaries of Diamond Bar, but it had been a long time since anyone had tried to make a go of it here.

Jeffrey hadn't.

Why had the man come back? What had he wanted the five thousand for? Some of it, according to Culpepper had been used to reclaim the old homestead against back taxes.

But he hadn't wanted to stay here when his folks were alive. Why had he come back when they were dead?

And why would anyone want this worthless spread now, when no one had wanted it before?

Going back to celebrate my birthday, Jeffrey had told Lassiter. *Rob a bank, kill a man, rape a woman...*

A joke? A man soured by prison life, sounding off? Or—an old hurt? Revenge?

Lassiter rode to the rim of a hill, looked off. The land sloped away here toward the Gila, too far away to be seen. The Santa Fe Junction was out there somewhere. There was good land out there, graze, cattle. But not here, not in these stony, forbidding hills.

The sun was going down, the shadows beginning to creep down from the higher slopes. But the wind that brushed against Lassiter was warmer...one of those odd quirks of weather in this part of the country. It was still January, but a warming trend was setting in. Lassiter knew it wouldn't last.

Lassiter, cattle baron!

He made a wry face. What the hell, he wasn't cut out for this anyway.

He swung down off the hill, heading back toward the ranch. The slopes and the hills around him were spotted with old mine shafts, tailings weathered, ore buckets rusted, hanging precariously above brush-choked canyons.

Lassiter was cutting away along the base of the ridge that separated him from the ranchhouse when something caught his eye. He turned the roan to it, dismounted, walked to what looked like an old well, its stone rim recently remortared, a bucket still hanging from a windlass.

Lassiter put his hands on the stone rim, looked down. Shadows hid the bottom of the well. He turned, picked up a fist-sized rock, dropped it. He counted slowly to six before he heard the rock hit the bottom. A faint, hollow clack...not in water, not even in mud!

There had never been water in this well, never would be! No place for a well, anyway...

A rock, Lassiter remembered from somewhere, falls about sixteen feet a second. He figured the shaft as about one hundred feet deep.

A long way to dig for water in a place even an Iowa farmer would know was futile...

The rope holding the bucket was weathered...didn't look long enough to reach the bottom. It was still good enough to hold the bucket, but wouldn't hold a man. The stones making up the rim of the well had not been long laid, and the mortar was barely beginning to show signs of crumbling.

Lassiter leaned over the rim for another look down into the well—

The bullet missed him by inches, slammed into the oak bucket, went through it, died among the rocks on the far slope.

Lassiter was around, two long strides bringing him to his ground-picketed roan as the rifle crack sounded a split second later, a faint pop in the distance.

He jerked his rifle free from its saddle scabbard, levered a shell into place, looked back down the stony canyon.

He had a glimpse of a figure ducking back...a shadow...

Tuy Song?

Lassiter wasn't sure. But someone didn't want him looking around here...someone ready to kill him.

CHAPTER SIXTEEN

Laura was standing in the doorway when Lassiter rode into the yard. It was almost too dark to see her, but there was a light inside the ranchhouse and through the window Lassiter could see Tuy Song bending over a cooking pot by the fireplace.

"Lassiter!" Laura ran out to meet him. "What happened? I heard a shot—"

"A rabbit," Lassiter said, his tone casual. "Missed him."

He went into the barn, stripped his saddle from the roan. Laura followed him inside. She looked genuinely frightened.

"I thought Carradine...or one of his men..."

"He gave us forty-eight hours," Lassiter said. "I don't think he'll be back before then..."

She shivered a little. "I don't know...I don't trust him. I don't know why he'd want this place." She looked up into Lassiter's face. "I don't know what I'd do if something happened to you..."

Lassiter turned the roan loose inside a stall and looked in on the steeldust. The animal was restless, nervous. He didn't belong here.

Laura's voice was steadier now. "What did you find out there?"

"A lot of old mine shafts, a couple of graves—and a well."

Laura's brow puckered. "A well?"

"Yeah," Lassiter said, watching her. "Didn't you know?"

"No. The only water we have, far as I know, is from the spring..."

"Jeffrey never mentioned it?"

"Jeffrey told me very little about the ranch," Laura answered. "I knew about the two graves, his father and mother. He seemed quite bitter about it."

They went outside. It was getting dark. Brutus came into the yard from somewhere in those cold and arid hills. He paused, eyeing Lassiter.

"Don't you ever tie him up?" Lassiter asked.

"Sometimes," Laura said. "Mostly I let him run loose. He's the only protection I have...besides you now," she amended.

They went inside the ranchhouse. Whatever was cooking in one of those black iron pots hanging in the fireplace smelled good.

Tuy Song was setting plates on the trestle table. He didn't look at Lassiter.

Laura reached under the sink, pulled out a copper boiler.

"Be a few minutes yet before supper," she said. "I think I'll take a bath."

Lassiter eyed the boiler. "In that?"

"Do you have anything better?" she asked. She

motioned to a big bucket of water set on the hearth. "Should be warm enough. Would you?"

He picked up the bucket, followed her into the bedroom. She poured the tepid water into the boiler, started to undress.

Lassiter watched her. She stopped.

"I'm taking a bath," she said.

"Sure. Go right ahead."

"Alone." Then she sighed. "Please?"

He nodded, went back into the bigger room. She drew the curtain tightly across the bedroom doorway behind him.

Tuy Song was watching him from across the table, his hands tucked inside his sleeves. Eyes bland, face inscrutable. Thirty, maybe older. Couldn't tell about these yellow-skinned bastards.

Lassiter walked to the fireplace. Laura's rifle was propped against the stones, same place it had been before he had ridden out.

Lassiter picked up the rifle, sniffed at the muzzle. It had been fired recently, the faint smell of gunpowder remaining.

He levered a shell into the firing chamber, turned the muzzle to Tuy Song.

The man flinched, eyes suddenly black almond pools. "What's down there?" Lassiter asked. His voice was low, casual, edged with steel.

The pigtailed Chinaman stared impassively. "Velly solly," he hissed, "not know what you say —"

-Lassiter rammed the muzzle into his lean stomach. "That old well behind the ridge? What's down there?"

Tuy Song eyes glittered, fear showing. "You kill Tuy Song—?"

"Why not?"

"You kill me, Lassiter," Tuy Song said, "and you'll lose whatever chance you have of finding out..."

He was desperate, and in his desperation he forgot to play the dumb Chinaman, the humble Orientle speaking a sort of pidgin English.

Lassiter's grin was edged. "Sorry, Song. But I think I already know—"

"Lassiter!"

Lassiter turned his head. Laura was standing in the bedroom doorway, stark naked, streaks of soap clinging to her.

The picture of her caught Lassiter, held him for a fraction of a second, and nearly cost him his life.

He jerked back in time to spin away from the knife in Tuy Song's hand, felt it slice through his coat, burn down his back.

He brought the butt of the Winchester up under Song's chin, smashing bone and teeth, sending the Chinaman stumbling back. Lassiter fired then, the bullet pinning Song to the old floor boards. He fired once more and Song jerked, then slowly relaxed, the knife slipping from his curled fingers.

Lassiter turned, jacking another shell into the Winchester's chamber.

Laura was staring across the room, face white, voice strained. "You killed him?"

Lassiter nodded, walked to her.

She shrank back from the look on his face, the rifle in his hands.

"Lassiter...no...."

"You put him up to it," Lassiter growled.

She rolled her head from side to side. "Why should I?"

"He took a shot at me out there," Lassiter growled. "While I was checking out that well. You sent him after me..."

"Lassiter—I swear. I didn't...I wouldn't..." She was backed up against the bed now. A hand came up under a breast, cupped it, the nipple stiffening.

She ran the tip of her tongue across her red lips. "I need *you*, Lassiter...not him. We're partners, aren't we? Fifty-fifty...?"

There was a burning across his back, where Song's knife had cut, but there was a greater fire in his loins, a stiffening between his legs.

Laura saw it, licked her lips, eyes shining. "Just you and me, Lassiter..."

It was the one weakness in Lassiter, the flaw in the hard armor he had wrapped around his life. He was a sucker for a woman, he always had been, and some day it would be his undoing.

Laura lay back on the bed, waiting, sure of herself now.

"Lassiter," she said shoftly, "hurry. It's cold..."

He put the rifle aside and went to her.

CHAPTER SEVENTEEN

Lassiter buried Tuy Song close to the graves of Jeffrey Bannock's parents. He wrestled a heavy rock to the head of the shallow grave, set Tuy Song's Buddha on it and lighted one last incense stick as an epitaph to Song's departure.

Laura watched him, with Brutus by her side. The big, half-wild dog was sitting on his haunches, tongue lolling, an occasional low growl coming from him. He trusted no one save Laura. He barely tolerated Lassiter.

Lassiter leaned on his shovel, looked toward the surrounding hills. The sun was already beginning to warm the land, sucking the shadows back from the silent hills.

There were hundreds of Chinese buried around forgotten mining camps, most of them in common, unmarked graves. Small, yellow-skinned men who had come here looking for gold or silver, for a better life than they had at home...second-class citizens to the men already here—heathens not worthy of proper burial.

Life was cheap enough in the mining camps—an

Oriental's worth nothing at all.

But Tuy Song had been different from most of his smuggled-in countrymen. He had not left when the others had. He had taken work at the Diamond Bar after Jeffrey returned, and stayed after Jeffrey died.

Lassiter let his gaze drift toward the ridge behind which a deep well had been dug and abandoned. He needed a rope long enough to reach down to the bottom of it, and the only place he could find one was in town.

He had twenty-four hours to find what was down in that well...twenty-four hours to find what made this rundown ranch valuable to Carradine...and to the Judge.

Sidney Blood was already on his way here. Sidney Blood, and half a dozen Wells Fargo agents.

If he worked it right he could be a long way to Tampico before they got here.

He walked back to the ranchhouse with Laura, saddled his roan.

"I'm going into town," he told her. "Want to come along?"

She shook her head, but there was fear in her eyes. "You leaving?"

He shrugged. "There's nothing here," he said. "I think I'll take the Judge's offer, ride on out—"

"You can't do that!" she cried. "What about me? Where will I go?"

Brutus sensed her distress. He got to his feet and took a few steps toward Lassiter, a warning rumble in his throat.

Lassiter dropped his hand to his gun butt. The dog crouched, waiting.

"Come with me," he told her. "We can have a good time in Tampico with five thousand dollars."

"And then what?" She shook her head, eyes brimming with tears. "I'm staying here."

"The Judge'll be taking over," Lassiter reminded her.

"I don't care! I've held off Carradine...I'll hold him off, too!"

Lassiter shrugged. "Good luck," he said, and rode off.

Laura waited until Lassiter was out of sight on the road to Rimrock, then she went into the barn, saddled the chestnut, rode out to the well behind the ridge, and looked down into its dark depths.

It was a long way down. But Tuy Song had followed Lassiter here yesterday, tried to kill him. Not on her orders. Why? Had the yellow sonofabitch known where the money was hidden? Had he been holding out on her?

She didn't have much time. If Lassiter sold out to the Judge, like he said...

The shots trembled on the stillness...faint, distant. Pulled her away from the well, into saddle, fear drawing her mouth tight. She was alone here, vulnerable...

She rode back to the ranchhouse, pulled up, a gasp choking her.

"Brutus!"

She dismounted, ran to him, lying motionless in

119

the dust of the yard, blood from the bullet holes matting his short hair.

A small wind ruffled Brutus' hide as she touched the still head. This dog had been the only real friend Laura had.

She heard a horse snort behind her and she turned, ran to the chestnut, reaching for the rifle jutting from the saddle scabbard—

The bullet was meant as a warning..a flat, echoing sound, missing her by a foot, freezing her.

She turned.

Carradine was sitting in saddle, a gun in his hand, smoke leaking from the muzzle. There was another Pitchfork rider with him, a slim, red-haired man with tawny eyes.

"Saw that gunslinger, Lassiter, ride out. Figured you'd be around somewhere." Carradine eased his gun back into holster. "Where's that slant-eyed cook of yours?"

"Inside..." Laura lied.

Carradine dismounted, walked to her, jerked her around, away from the chestnut.

"We looked," he said roughly. "Where is he?"

Laura shook her head. "I don't know. I thought he was—"

Carradine slapped her, snapping her head back, bringing tears to her eyes.

"Take a look around," he said to his companion. "If you find him, kill him!"

The man nodded, swung his horse around, rode out of the yard.

Carradine turned back to Laura. "Where is it?"

She feigned innocence. "I don't know what you're talking about—"

He slapped her again, bringing blood to her mouth. "The money," he said harshly. "One hundred and fifty thousand dollars Jeffrey stole..."

She raised a hand to her mouth: "Dave...please...I don't know—"

He hit her again and she sank to her knees, sobbing. He stood over her, waiting.

"It's here somewhere. That's why you came back. You knew about the money—"

He grabbed her by the hair, jerked her to her feet. "We searched this place inside out after Jeffrey died," Carradine snarled. "Goddam Chink kept out of sight—"

He turned as the redhaired rider came back.

"The Chink's dead," the man said. He was a cold, emotionless man who had hired on at Pitchfork shortly after Dave took over. He waved. "New-dug grave back there, close by a couple of old ones. Heathen statue on it."

Dave turned back to Laura. "Who killed him?"

"Lassiter." The name came reluctantly from her lips. She licked her lips, backed off from Carradine. "I don't know where Jeffrey hid the money...he never told me. But I think Tuy Song knew...."

Dave exchanged a look with the redhaired rider. The man shrugged.

"The Chink's dead," he said tonelessly.

Carradine ground his teeth in frustration. He had come back to Pitchfork after his father died only because he was broke and had nowhere else to go. He had lived high for a while on the money his father had given him, then drifted into gambling for a living. He didn't give a hang about Pitchfork—he would have sold it the day he got back, if he had had a decent offer.

One hundred and fifty thousand dollars would put him back into the style of living he wanted.

He walked to Laura, pressed back against the ranchhouse wall, drew his gun, cocked it, jammed the muzzle between her breasts.

"I made a fair offer for this fleabag spread!" he said. "I'm not leaving without it!"

"Then you'll have to stop Lassiter," Laura said. "He's riding into town to sell Diamond Bar to the Judge!"

Carradine stiffened. "The Judge?"

Laura nodded. "Lassiter doesn't know about the money. The Judge made him an offer yesterday, and he's going to take it. He's not coming back."

Carradine whirled around to the redhaired rider. "Take my horse, Flint—he's faster than yours. I want Lassiter stopped before he gets to town. Kill him!"

Flint didn't move.

"He's got a half-hour start on you!" Carradine snarled. "Move!"

The redhaired man leaned forward over his saddle horn. "How much, Carradine?"

Carradine stared at him, eyes burning.

"I get paid fifty a month for riding range,"

Flint said. "Killing a man is worth more."

Carradine nodded. "How much do you want?"

"Five thousand dollars, payable when I get back."

Carradine hesitated. It was more money than he had available without selling Pitchfork. But if that goddam phony Judge got legal title to Diamond Bar—

Flint waited, eyes cold.

"All right," Carradine snarled. "Five thousand.. But not till I know for sure you've stopped him!"

"Fair enough," Flint replied.

He swung out of saddle, taking his rifle with him as he walked to Carradine's big black stallion. Drawing Carradine's fancy Winchester from the saddle boot, he tossed it to Dave, slipped his own rifle in its place. He mounted, swung around, waved.

"Be back before sundown."

Carradine watched him ride off before turning to Laura.

"We'll wait inside."

She saw the look in his eyes, knew what it meant. She had been that route before.

She turned, walked into the house ahead of him.

CHAPTER EIGHTEEN

Culpepper choked on the whiskey bottle tilted to his lips, stared with shocked, frightened gaze at the gun in Lassiter's hand.

"Jesus!"

Liquor dribbled down his chin, made a wet streak down his gravy-stained waistcoat. He shrank back against his desk, jowls quivering, as Lassiter kicked the door shut behind him and walked toward Culpepper.

"How'd it go?" Lassiter asked. He had his thumb on the spiked hammer, his voice easy but not friendly.

"Go? Christ! Put that thing away! You want to scare a man to death...?"

Lassiter grinned, teeth showing, no humor in it. "Well?"

Culpepper took courage at the fact that Lassiter hadn't shot him. He put the bottle down on his desk and spread his hands in oratorical gesture.

"I just got back. Everything has been taken care of for you. Title's cleared, will probated. You own the Diamond Bar..."

"That fast, eh?"

Culpepper nodded. "If you know how..." He sank down into his padded chair, his knees still weak from shock. "Grease a few palms, Lassiter..."

"With what?" Lassiter said. "I thought you needed money."

Culpepper wet his lips. "I had a little. You said you'd pay me as soon as you sold the place."

Lassiter figured the old windbag was lying. But it didn't matter. He wasn't hanging around long.

"What about Laura Bannock?"

"Laura?"

"Yeah, Jeffrey's wife. You wrote to her telling her Jeffrey was dead. You knew she'd come back."

Culpepper sighed. "Kinda slipped my mind, Lassiter..."

Lassiter reached down, grabbed Culpepper by his dirty celluloid collar, jerked him to his feet, slammed him up against the wall.

"You told that phony Judge about my loaning Jeffrey five thousand dollars?"

Culpepper's gaze darted around the room like a pregnant doe caught in a forest fire. "You said you wanted to sell. I told him you'd probably take what Jeffrey owed you."

Lassiter let up on him, frowned.

"What sort of deal did you make?"

Culpepper smoothed out his waistcoat, regained his composure. "Deal? My good man, there's a matter of professional ethics involved here—"

Lassiter's gun muzzle nicked his whiskey-veined nose.

"How much, shyster?"

The attorney licked his lips. "Ten percent commission. Payable when you sell..."

"Five thousand dollars," Lassiter said. "Cheap enough for a ranch worth a hundred and fifty thousand, eh, Culpepper?"

The fat man stared at him. "A hundred and fifty—" He broke off, shook his head, sighed. "I see you've heard about the money that's supposed to be buried somewhere on Diamond Bar?"

"It's there," said Lassiter. "Down an old well on the other side of the ridge."

Culpepper's gaze flickered, went sad. "Guess you fell for it, too, Lassiter. Tuy Song started it. Guess Jeffrey put him up to it. Jeffrey helped it along..."

Lassiter scowled. "He didn't rob that bank?"

Culpepper shrugged. "That's what a lot of people thought, especially when it got out that the bank manager was the same clerk Jeffrey had had trouble with years ago. The sheriff looked around, so did a couple of Federal men. They didn't find anything. And they couldn't hold Jeffrey, not with the bank's books showing Goodson, the bank manager, had been embezzling..."

Lassiter eased his gun back into the holster, reached for the bottle. Wasn't every day a man lost a hundred and fifty thousand dollars.

"Why did Jeffrey pass the word around that he had the money?"

Culpepper shrugged. "That came later, after things quieted down. Right after his wife left. Seems to me he was ready to sell...maybe he had had enough of the place. Letting folks think the money was buried on his spread boosted up the price..."

"Did it?"

Culpepper nodded. "Not at first. Nobody believed him. Hell, if he had that much money stashed away, why didn't he pick it up and get out?"

"Makes sense," Lassiter growled.

"But Jeffrey was a strange man," Culpepper went on. "And a shrewd one. He told me himself there wasn't any money. He was ready to sell as soon as somebody came up with a decent offer. He had Dave Carradine believing it. Then he was killed..."

Lassiter walked away from Culpepper, to the window, looked down on the street.

"Take the Judge's money," Culpepper said. He chuckled. "Let him and Carradine fight it out. Five thousand dollars is more than you came in with, Lassiter."

Lassiter nodded.

The attorney reached into a pigeonhole on his desk, took out an official-looking envelope. "Deed to Diamond Bar," he said. "It's yours."

"What about Laura Bannock?"

Culpepper plucked at his nose. "A beautiful woman...she'll get along. I'm sorry about Tuy Song, though..."

Lassiter swung away from the window just as Flint, leading a limping black horse, came by. Flint glanced at Lassiter's roan tied up at the rack in front of Culpepper's office, broke stride for a moment, then moved on.

"Tuy Song's dead," Lassiter said. "I killed him." He picked up the envelope, glanced at the deed inside. It looked legal, official seals and all.

"Cost me fifty dollars," Culpepper grumbled.

"Take it out of your commission from the Judge," Lassiter said.

He opened the door, stepped outside. Somehow the wind seemed colder than usual. From where he stood he could see the snow on Tejon Peak, the clouds piling up behind it. Snow would be a foot high around here, any day now.

He pulled his collar up around his ears, walked down the long flight of stairs, turned the corner and stopped.

Christ! Not again!

Marshal Winters' big Peacemaker's muzzle was an inch from his nose. Behind it the marshal loomed bigger, meaner—the truce was off!

Winters grinned. "Got a better offer, Lassiter," he said. "From the Judge."

Lassiter shrugged. What the hell. He was going there anyway.

CHAPTER NINETEEN

Flint hunkered down against the wall, watching the blacksmith hammer a cold shoe onto the black's left hind leg. He waited patiently, running possibilities through his mind, knowing he wouldn't be going back to Pitchfork. He had not wanted to, anyway.

He had asked for five thousand dollars, but he had not expected to get it from Dave Carradine. A bullet most likely, but no money.

The black throwing a shoe had delayed him, cut off all chance of catching up with Lassiter on the trail. He shifted his weight, ground out his cigarette butt as the blacksmith said: "Got a stone bruise, too...not bad. But ride him easy for a while..."

Flint nodded. "Mister Carradine's horse," he said. He didn't have to say it; the blacksmith knew the big black with the Pitchfork brand well enough, but Flint made it sound concerned. "He'll pay you next time he's in town."

He led the black out of the blacksmith's shop, mounted, swung down the street in time to see

Lassiter go inside the Territorial Bar with Marshal Winters.

He waited a moment, checking his possibilities. There were only two roads out of Rimrock: one back through the high pass to the Jurado House and points beyond, the other east toward the Santa Fe Junction.

Lassiter would be taking one or the other when he sold out to the Judge. Whichever way he took, Flint figured to be ready for him.

L. C. Spellman sat waiting behind his desk as Lassiter stepped inside with Marshal Winters at his back. The big man closed the door behind him, said: "No trouble, Judge. He wants to talk to you."

There were two other men inside the room. One of them had a skinning knife in his hands. He was paring his dirty nails with it.

Spellman hooked his right thumb inside a corner of his vest, leaned back in his chair.

"You had your chance," he said coldly. "I'm through talking, Lassiter."

Lassiter shrugged. "I thought you were still interested in buying Diamond Bar. That's why I came back."

Spellman studied him, running this through his mind. "Not any more," he said, his tone indifferent.

Lassiter looked disappointed. "I've got the deed to Diamond Bar right here," he said, tapping his coat pocket. "Picked it up in Culpepper's office...I was coming to see you when the marshal showed up..."

Spellman leaned forward, avarice gleaming briefly in his gaze. "You're worth five thousand to me right now, Lassiter. All I have to do is hold you until Sidney Blood gets here."

Lassiter shrugged. "I thought of that. You'll get the reward money, but you won't get Diamond Bar."

He was gambling that the Judge believed in the hundred and fifty thousand dollars.

Spellman let Lassiter wait for a long moment, then he leaned back again, a thin smile showing.

"I offered you five thousand yesterday," he said. "Why didn't you take it then?"

"Wanted to hold out a while longer," Lassiter answered. "Figgered if you were willing to pay me that much for Diamond Bar, Carradine might go higher."

The Judge's eyes glittered. "How much higher?"

Lassiter shrugged. "Haven't had time to find out. You've got me treed. I can't hang around here dickering, not with Sidney Blood on the way."

Spellman smiled. "Now you're showing sense, Lassiter."

He got up, walked to a small safe, opened it, took out the big envelope into which he had put the money, set it down on his desk.

"Count it," he said casually, putting the bill of sale down beside the envelope. "Five thousand dollars."

Lassiter looked at the two men Spellman had waiting in the room. They had moved apart, were waiting behind him. Only Winters looked puzzled.

Lassiter was not surprised. The Judge figured to get Diamond Bar and the reward money.

"Sign it," the Judge said, "and the money is yours."

Lassiter moved to the desk. "Why do you want the Bannock spread? You already own a ranch."

Spellman ran the tip of his finger down the bridge of his nose. "Lots of old mines out there," he said. "I'm a gambler. One of them might pan out rich...."

Yeah, Lassiter thought, *one hundred and fifty thousand dollars worth!*

"You're more of a gambler than I am," Lassiter conceded. He took out the deed to Diamond Bar, tossed it on the desk. "Hope you have better luck with it than I had..."

He picked up the quill pen from its holder, leaned over the bill of sale. Spellman watched him. It was very quiet in the office.

Lassiter started to sign. He was watching Spellman as he finished with a flourish. The man's eyes gave him away.

Lassiter whirled, ducking as he spun away. The skinning knife missed him by inches and buried its razor-sharp point in Spellman's throat.

Lassiter killed the man who had thrown it, smashed a bullet into the gun arm of the other, held his gun on the marshal.

Winters hadn't made a move.

Lassiter reached back, picked up the envelope, tucked it inside his coat, under his belt. The Judge was staring at them, eyes wide, glazing, one hand clutched at his throat, blood spurting through his fingers. He would be dead before Lassiter made it to the street.

"Turn around!" Lassiter said to Winters.

Winters obeyed, in a daze.

Lassiter palmed his Colt. "Sorry about the whorehouse, Marshal," he murmured. "Maybe another time..." He slugged the big man across the back of his head, stepped over him as Winters went down like a felled ox.

No one bothered him as Lassiter went outside, walked up the street to his picketed roan. He mounted, swung away from the rack, looked back to Culpepper's window. He thought he glimpsed the attorney watching him, but he wasn't sure.

He had the five thousand dollars he had loaned Jeffrey Bannock. It was enough to get him to Tampico, rest up, let his wounds heal.

He turned the roan west, toward the high pass through which he had come three days earlier.

CHAPTER TWENTY

Flint waited for Lassiter high up in the rocks of Tejon Pass. The wind blowing through the canyon was cold, and it would get colder. Storm clouds were blotting out the sun.

Flint cradled his Winchester, blew on his cold hands. Carradine's black stallion was picketed further back in a hollow shielded by jackpine. There was no way Lassiter could spot him from the trail below.

A hawk came gliding down the north rim, swooped low over the rocky slope, its sharp, raucous cry intended to startle into movement any rock squirrel fool enough to have come out of its hole to enjoy the sun. He glided along the slope, then dipped across the canyon and went up over the rim behind Flint.

The Pitchfork rider stared down on the trail, at a point where a jut of rock hid it from further view. Lassiter should be coming around that bend just about now....

He eased his rifle muzzle across the top of the boulder, sighted down the barrel. The slopes flanking the Pass at this point were not too steep, boulder strewn, dotted with brush and jackpine. But the rims were sheer, unclimbable.

No way Lassiter could get back past him. No way!

Lassiter was thinking about Tampico and worrying about the gathering storm as he came down the trail through Tejon Pass. He might get as far as the Jurado House before it broke; he didn't like the idea of being holed up at the trail house. Not with Sidney Blood behind him.

His thoughts drifted to Laura Bannock. It would have been fun having her along. It was a long way to Tampico.

He came around a bend in the road, the slopes falling away now, the canyon widening. The roan blew noisily, arching its neck. It was tired, sides heaving, steam rising from its flanks, dissipating in the cold air.

Lassiter pulled up. The animal wouldn't last to Tampico. Maybe he could pick up a horse at the Jurado House. Fresco had to have an animal somewhere.

He leaned forward over the saddle horn, letting the roan blow. He wanted a smoke, but his fingers were too cold.

Then he stiffened, a barely perceptible movement, as his gaze picked up a hoofprint just ahead, sharp-etched into a slab of trail slate. Fresh grooves made not too long ago...made by someone riding just ahead of him!

Then Lassiter sensed the muzzle trained on him. He knew it instinctively. He had been hunted too long.

The hawk came back over the cliff rim, dipped down the slope, shied abruptly away as it spotted Flint below, its cry sharp, warning...

Flint cursed as he fired.

Lassiter was already falling forward out of saddle and away from the man on the south slope. Flint's bullet plucked at his coat, snarled off rocks on the far side of the canyon trail.

Lassiter landed on his hands and knees, whirled to make a grab for the rifle in his saddle boot. But the roan jerked away, snorting. It started to run just as Flint's next slug hit him, ripping through his left shoulder. The roan went down, legs thrashing.

Lassiter had no chance for the rifle pinned under the dying animal. He made a run up the opposite slope, seeking cover. He staggered as a bullet ripped the heel from his right boot, fell forward, rolled behind a boulder as Flint's next two slugs whined off rocks just ahead of him.

Lassiter emptied his Colt blindly toward the rocks high up on the opposite slope. The distance was too great for a handgun, but it made Flint duck down momentarily, and allowed Lassiter to make it to a rock burst further up the slope. A bullet powdered rock a few inches from his face as he dove behind it.

Lassiter crouched, looked down the pass to the roan dead on the trail, ran his gaze up the other slope to a point where gunsmoke drifting away from rock's pinpointed his ambusher.

His rifle was down there with the roan. He had a Colt against a rifle, and it didn't look good.

Flint took his time reloading his Winchester. He had Lassiter trapped with the north rim at his back. He could pick Lassiter off any time Lassiter tried to make a break for it.

But there was a storm brewing and Flint knew what it could be like to be trapped in Tejon Pass by a blizzard.

He stood up, knowing Lassiter couldn't reach him with a hand gun, cupped his hands to his mouth:

"Lassiter! You can't make it out of here! Let's make a deal!"

His voice bounced back from the far rim, faded in ragged mutterings down canyon.

"What do you say, Lassiter?"

Flint ducked back behind his rock as Lassiter's shot spattered harmlessly below him. It had been an instinctive reaction and for good measure he laid a couple of slugs into the rock nest where Lassiter was hiding.

The wind sharpened, soughed through the jackpine. Lassiter considered. He didn't know who the rifleman was, had figured him for a bounty hunter who had learned of the Wells Fargo reward.

He looked behind him. The cliff was scalable, but he'd be picked off like a fly on a wall if he tried it. He could chance making a run down to the roan to get his hands on his rifle...but it was a long shot he would chance only when he had no other choice.

He cupped his hands to his mouth, yelled across the canyon: "What do you want?"

Flint grinned, his eyes bleak. He had him.

"Give me the money the Judge paid you for Diamond Bar and I'll ride out of here!"

Lassiter frowned. How had he found out about the money? One of the Judge's men? Someone who had known he'd be heading this way—?"

"What do you say, Lassiter?"

Lassiter's face was grim. He was counting on that money and didn't intend to hand it over to some passing ambusher.

He slid his Colt into holster, reached for his belly gun tucked into a small pocket sewn in his underwear. A small, double-barreled derringer, .30 caliber, over and under barrels. Two shots. Had to get close up with it, though.

He rubbed the tip of his nose. Might work. What other chance did he have?"

"All right!" he yelled back. "The money's in my saddle bag. Go down and get it!"

Flint sneered. What did Lassiter take him for—a tinhorn fool? The dead roan was within range of Lassiter's Colts.

He stood up, rifle held across his waist. "We'll go down together," he said. "Come on out, Lassiter!"

Lassiter watched him. A nervous, frightened man he would have distrusted. But this man knew how to handle a rifle; he was sure of himself. He'd

141

play with Lassiter a while before killing him.

Would he wait long enough?

Lassiter stepped out from behind the rocks, his hands in the air, and started down the slope toward the trail.

Flint grinned. He started to raise his rifle, then paused. Maybe Lassiter was lying about the money being in the saddle bag. What if he had hidden it up there somewhere?

He yelled: "Far enough, Lassiter! Unbuckle your gun belts! Drop them!"

Lassiter eased his hands down, let his cartridge belts drop down at his feet. He raised his hands again, and clasped them across his hat.

"We made a deal," he yelled to Flint. "The money's there in those saddle bags!"

Flint went down the slope, his eyes locked on Lassiter coming down the other side. He beat Lassiter to the trail, stood over the roan, sneered: "Far enough, Lassiter!"

Lassiter paused a scant twenty feet away, his hands on his head.

Flint knelt beside the dead horse, reached inside the saddle bag. He kept his eyes on Lassiter as he pulled the envelope out.

"I told you the money was there," Lassiter said.

Flint had the rifle muzzle levelled at him...he took his eyes away from Lassiter to look into the envelope, and Lassiter's right hand jerked away from under his hat, the derringer like a toy in it.

Flint reacted too late, came up from his crouch as the first .30 caliber slug hit him in the chest, hit bone, deflected into his heart. Lassiter's second shot wasn't necessary.

Flint fell backward, his finger closing spasmodically on the rifle trigger, the shot going into the air, the echoes bouncing from the canyon walls.

Lassiter crouched, pulled the rifle away from the man's nerveless fingers, looked down into Flint's hard face.

"How'd you know?" he asked grimly. "Who sent you?"

Flint's eyes were glazing. He was dying. What the hell, he didn't owe Carradine anything.

"Carradine..." he said. Lassiter had to bend close to hear. "At Diamond Bar...waiting..."

He sighed then, closed his eyes.

So Carradine was waiting, Lassiter thought bleakly. *Well, let him wait!*

He picked up Flint's rifle, went back up the slope for his gunbelts, strapped them on.

Carradine was a fool, like the Judge had been...he thought Jeffrey had the bank money, had it hidden somewhere on Diamond Bar. Even Laura Bannock had believed it...

Lassiter went back to the roan, picked up the envelope. He grinned. *A bird in the hand,* he figured, mixing his metaphors, *was worth a hell of a lot more than a hundred and fifty thousand dollars that never was.*

The small packets were inside, the way he had seen them. He took one out, peeled off the fifty-dollar bill. He stared at the cigar coupon below it.

It was the same with the others. Five packets of money—five fifty-dollar bills, wrapped around worthless cigar coupons.

Two hundred and fifty dollars! Lassiter couldn't make Tampico on that, not in the style he wanted.

The wind blew colder down the canyon pass. He felt it bite through his coat, chill him.

The Judge had outfoxed him. He had showed him the money, but had never intended Lassiter to get his hands on it.

Going back to rob a bank, kill a man, rape a woman....

Jeffrey's parting words echoed in Lassiter's head. To hell with what Culpepper had said...it fitted! All of it. Laura Bannock refusing to leave...Tuy Song trying to head him away from the old well...

The bank money *was* there, all one hundred and fifty thousand dollars of it. Real money, not cigar store coupons. And Laura knew where it was. It was still there, if Carradine hadn't beaten it out of her by now.

Lassiter shoved the fifties into his pocket, scattered the coupons to the wind. He went up the slope carrying Flint's rifle. Flint had a horse picketed somewhere. Lassiter knew he'd find it.

CHAPTER TWENTY-ONE

Carradine was getting anxious. Flint should have been back by now. He walked to the window, looked out across the yard to the road leading to Rimrock. The clouds piling up over the mountains looked ominous. Could be blowing a blizzard by nightfall...

Behind him Laura huddled by the fireplace, mouth bloodied, eyes hurt, dazed. She whimpered and he looked back at her, a sneer on his thin face.

She'd come around eventually—they all did.

He went back to her, pulled her to her feet, shoved her toward the bedroom. She stared at him, her body numb.

She didn't know why she had held out on Carradine. The money no longer mattered. But some inner stubbornness prevailed, held her mute through the brutal assaults he had forced on her, the cruel indignities.

She was not a virgin; she had had men before, some rough, some tender. But Carradine was brutal.

He pushed her ahead of him, into the bedroom...she stumbled back against the bedpost, started to undress...

Carradine set his rifle against the wall by the doorway, unbuckled his belt. It was wide, thick, with a heavy, inlaid silver buckle. He wrapped one end of the belt around his fist, letting the buckle dangle.

"Some women like being hurt," Carradine said. "Maybe this will soften you up—"

Laura shrank back from him, terror growing. "No...oh, please...no! The money...I think I know—"

Carradine was walking toward her...he paused, looked back as he heard a horse come into the ranchyard. The horse was moving slowly; it seemed to be limping.

Flint?

Carradine dropped his belt, picked up his rifle, went to the door.

His black stallion had stopped by the water trough. It was drinking thirstily. There was no one in saddle.

Carradine called: "Flint?"

The horse raised his head, looked at him...he whinnied, recognizing Carradine, began to limp across the yard...

Carradine stepped outside to meet him. He caught a glimpse of Lassiter coming around the far side of the house, and whirled. Lassiter's slug slammed him back. He rolled over once, shuddered at Lassiter's second shot, went limp.

The black shied off, limping. It did not run far.

146

Lassiter went into the house, into the bedroom. Laura was still standing by the bedpost, nude, shivering. She saw Lassiter come in, but it took a moment for it to register. Then:

"Lassiter...oh, thank God, Lassiter...."

He went to her as her knees buckled...he held her up, held her against him, smoothed her hair back from her face.

"The money's there, isn't it?" he said softly. "Inside that old well?"

She nodded, sobbing, shivering: "Yes, yes...."

Laura swallowed her coffee, its warmth bringing some color back to her cheeks. She was dressed, ready to leave...she had no regrets.

Lassiter went to the door, looked up at the threatening sky. Be dark soon enough, and with it would come snow.

"We'll need a rope," he muttered. "A hundred feet of it, strong enough to hold a man's weight..."

He remembered he had gone to Rimrock with that in mind—he regretted now he had not followed through on it.

"There's rope in the barn," Laura said. She was still shaken by her ordeal, by the savage brutality of Carradine.

Lassiter shook his head. "I looked."

"In the hay where Tuy Song slept," Laura said. "I found it yesterday, while Song was following you. It surprised me. I didn't know why he wanted a rope, why he had hidden it..."

They went into the barn. The rope was there,

147

just as Laura said. And it looked long enough.

"Song must have found the money just before I came back. His people used to mine here...Song must have known every mine shaft and tunnel around. Wherever Jeffrey had hidden it, Song finally found it. My showing up surprised him. He dropped the money down that old well. It had been searched before, and he knew no one would look down there again. He played along with me, pretending he didn't know where the money was...then you showed up and he got desperate..."

Lassiter had saddled the Pitchfork steeldust while she talked. That was her explanation, but he didn't buy all of it. Not her part in it.

He hung Song's coiled rope from the steeldust's saddle horn, helped saddle Laura's big chestnut.

"Let's go," he said roughly. "Be dark soon. And I don't fancy going down into that shaft at night."

Laura led her chestnut outside, paused as she looked across the yard to where Carradine's body lay not too far from Brutus.

She turned, looked at Lassiter, needing reassurance. "Fifty-fifty, Lassiter?" Her voice quivered. She had been through hell these last hours. She couldn't stand any more. "Lassiter—promise?"

Lassiter shrugged.

"Let's go get the money."

The old well looked deeper, gloomier, as Lassiter looped one end of Song's rope around the sturdy windlass, knotted it, tested it. It would hold.

He dropped the loose end into the shaft, Laura watching, the horses picketed just behind them. He saw the rope slither down, all of it, then hang there waiting.

Lassiter turned to look at Laura. He was putting his life in her hands. How much did she want the money?

It was getting gray, the wind rising. Blue-black clouds were spilling down off the high mountains. They'd never make it back through Tejon Pass. There was only one other way to go.

He said: "I'll give a jerk on the rope when I hit bottom...two jerks after that means I've found the money."

She nodded.

Lassiter swung out over the well rim, fingers gripping the hemp rope. He felt his weight drag on his arms, his shoulders, a sharp twinge reopening the bullet wound. He gritted his teeth, wrapped a leg around the rope, started to ease himself down.

The well seemed bottomless. The darkness enclosed him almost as soon as he dipped below the rim. The unseen walls seemed to press in on him. The muscles in his arms knotted, strained. He paused, wrapping both legs around the rope to rest, looked up. Laura's face was above him, outlined in the well opening against the gray sky.

"Lassiter..." Her voice seemed to reverberate down the shaft; it sounded anxious.

"You all right?"

Lassiter didn't waste breath answering. He

started down again. It was going to be a hell of a climb going back up.

It seemed an eternity before his boots hit bottom. He made sure of his footing before letting go of the rope, tilting his head back for a look up. It was like staring up from the inside of a smoke stack. The well opening looked no bigger than a half-dollar. If Laura was saying anything, he couldn't hear it.

He jerked once on the rope, waited for Laura's answering pull. Then he lighted a match, looked around...he shied off, dropping his hand to his gun as something skittered away, off into a dark slanting side tunnel.

Lassiter grinned sheepishly, lighted another match. It was wider at the bottom, the side tunnel shored up by rotting timbers.

This was just another old mine shaft, he thought, rimmed at the top with a windlass and made to look like a well. Probably Jeffrey's doing, or Tuy Song's.

The canvas bag was there, lying across one of the fallen timbers at the mouth of the side tunnel. The name TERRITORIAL MINERS BANK was stenciled across it.

Lassiter burned three more matches checking its contents. No cigar store coupons this time. Neat stacks of bills, some old, some new, in varying denominations. It looked like a lot of money, a hundred and fifty thousand dollars worth.

Lassiter figured he would count it later.

He jerked twice on the rope, felt Laura's excited

answering pull. It was a hell of a long way up, but the canvas sack he slung over his shoulder and tied to his belt spurred him.

Laura was waiting for him, eyes shining. Lassiter topped the rim, slung the bag at her feet, hung over the side, getting his strength back while Laura ran her fingers through the money, making small, excited sounds.

The cold wind chilled the sweat on Lassiter's body...he swung down beside her, looked up at the darkening sky.

"How far to the Junction?"

"From here, about eight miles," Laura answered. "Due east..."

They stuffed the money into the saddle bags, dropped the canvas bag back into the well. Lassiter cut the rope, let it drop into the shaft beside the empty bank bag.

Be a while before anyone else came nosing around, he thought.

They made it to the Santa Fe Junction ahead of the storm. They hit the rails first, followed them toward lights in the distance, pulled up by the station.

Stock pens sided the rails beyond, empty now, quiet. The rail line came down from the north, headed south.

While Laura waited, holding his horse, Lassiter went into the station. There was a night clerk on duty, answering a message coming in over the wire. He signed off, turned as Lassiter approached.

Lassiter asked if there was a train due.

"Yeah, a special. Due in about a half-hour." The station man peered at Lassiter. "Rancher hereabouts?"

"Yeah," Lassiter said. "Taking a trip—me and my wife..."

The station man nodded. "Train doesn't usually stop here this time of year...not quite sure why it's making a stopover now. It's headed south for El Paso, connecting up with Southern Pacific going to New Orleans..."

Lassiter bought two tickets, and asked where he could get a shave.

"Hotel across the street," the man answered. "Run by Santa Fe. Barbershop, general store, rooms..."

Lassiter's respect for railroads went up a couple of notches. They sure didn't miss a bet.

While he was getting a shave, Laura bought some clothes for herself, an outfit for Lassiter, and a black pigskin bag to hold the money.

The train was just coming in when they returned to the station, its headlight slicing through the first gritty flakes whipping across the iron rails.

Lassiter and Laura waited on the platform, back in the shadows. The engine panted like a monster waiting to pounce. The lighted windows of the club car were inviting.

A stock car had been added to the passenger train. Men were leading saddled horses down a ramp, lanterns waving.

Lassiter edged over for a closer look. Sidney Blood was there, cursing, giving orders. He was mounted, his coat pulled up around his ears. He was folding his arms across his chest to keep warm.

The dozen Wells Fargo agents mounted, bunched up behind him, and rode off, headed for Rimrock.

Lassiter grinned. He had bought half a dozen expensive cigars in the hotel lobby; he stuck one in his mouth, lighted it, as he and Laura went into the club car.

It was going to be a warm, pleasant ride to El Paso.

SHOOTOUT AT SHIPROCK
By Lee O. Miller
PRICE: $1.75   T51630
CATEGORY: Western

FATHER AND SON FEUD!

Ray Bonham found himself smack in the middle of a feud between Marshal Lyle and Lyle's son. Ray would be needing his Colt .45 to help settle things, but he didn't know exactly which side of the law he'd be shooting at!

JIM STEEL #6: AZTEC GOLD
By Chet Cunningham

PRICE: $1.75   T51690
CATEGORY: Western

GOLD AND GUNTROUBLE!

When Steel mixed gold and women, he got only one thing—hot lead!

GUN GAMBLE
By Christian Kassel

PRICE: $1.95 T51701
CATEGORY: Western

MAD DAY IN MONUMENT!
Dan Moody was a hard-working, honest young man, who turned gun-crazy after meeting one man — Jesse James!

STARLOG PRESENTS
THE BROTHERS HILDEBRANDT'S
1982 Calendar

ATLANTIS: The Lost Continent. It has been the object of romantic fantasies for centuries. Now the renowned art team, *The Brothers Hildebrandt*, have created what could well be the most fantastic interpretation of this mythical land: *The Brothers Hildebrandt ATLANTIS 1982 Calendar*.

With thirteen original full-color paintings plus small black-and-white sketches, ATLANTIS comes alive with dinosaurs, beautiful heroines and sleek spaceships—a mystical blending of technology and simplicity in the artistic style that belongs only to the Hildebrandt's.

From their famous *Star Wars* poster, to the illustrations for the *Sword of Shanarra*, to their own illustrated novel, *Urshurak*—the *Brothers Hildebrandt* have become the most influential force on the science fiction and fantasy art scene. But it was their three J.R.R. Tolkien calendars that brought the Brothers their international following.

Starlog Press, the leading publisher of science fiction and fantasy, is proud to premiere the *Brothers Hildebrandt's* newest calendar, destined to become as legendary as Atlantis itself. This is more than simply a collector's item; it is an art treasure and a journey into fantasies limited in scope only by human imagination. Join Starlog Press and the *Brothers Hildebrandt* on this epic search.

13 original full-color paintings. $7.95

ORDER YOUR HILDEBRANDT "ATLANTIS" CALENDAR NOW!   ONLY $7.95

Send to:
STARLOG PRESS
HILDEBRANDT "ATLANTIS" CALENDAR
475 Park Avenue South   New York, NY 10016

I'm ordering ___ "ATLANTIS" calendars at $7.95 each...... $____
Postage at $1.50 *each* $____
TOTAL ENCLOSED: $____

NAME (Please print clearly)

ADDRESS

CITY

STATE   ZIP

Foreign customers add $4.06 for each calendar ordered, surface rate postage.
Allow 4 to 6 weeks for delivery. ONLY U.S., Australian and New Zealand funds accepted.

STARLOG photo guidebook

All Books in This Special Series
- Quality high-gloss paper,
- Big 8¼"x11" page format.
- Rare photos and valuable reference data.
- A must for every science fiction library!
- Available at Waldenbooks, B. Dalton Booksellers and other fine bookstores. Or order directly, using the coupon below.

SPACE ART $8.95
($13 for deluxe)
196 pages, full color

SCIENCE FICTION WEAPONS
$3.95
34 pages, full color

SPACESHIPS $2.95
34 pages, over 100 photos

Latest Releases

TV EPISODE GUIDES
Science Fiction, Adventure and Superheroes $7.95, 96 pages
A complete listing of 12 fabulous science fiction adventure or superhero series. Each chapter includes (a) complete plot synopses (b) cast and crew lists (c) dozens of rare photos, many in FULL COLOR.

TOYS & MODELS
$3.95, 34 Pages
A photo-filled guide to the fantastic world of toys and games. There's everything from Buck Rogers rocket skates to a mini Robby the Robot! Full-color photos showcase collections spanning four generations.

SPACESHIPS (new enlarged edition)
$7.95, 96 pages
The most popular book in the series has been expanded to three times the pages and updated with dozens of new photos from every movie and TV show that features spaceships-the dream machines! Many in full color.

HEROES $3.95, 34 pages
From Flash Gordon to Luke Skywalker, here is a thrilling photo scrapbook of the most shining heroes in science-fiction movies, TV and literature. Biographies of the men and women who inspire us and bring triumphant cheers from audiences.

FANTASTIC WORLDS $7.95
96 pages, over 200 photos

SPECIAL EFFECTS, VOL. I
$6.95, 96 pages, full color

SPECIAL EFFECTS, VOL. II
$7.95, 96 pages

VILLAINS $3.95
34 pages, full color

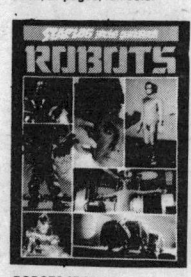

ROBOTS $7.95
96 pages, full color

ALIENS $7.95
96 pages, over 200 photos

Send to: STARLOG GUIDEBOOKS DEPT. FA3 475 Park Avenue South New York, NY 10016

Name

Address

City

State   Zip

— Add postage to your order: —

HEROES............$3.95	FANTASTIC WORLDS	SPACE ART
VILLAINS...........$3.95	................$7.95	Regular Edition....$8.95
SPACESHIPS I.....$2.95	ROBOTS............$7.95	Deluxe Edition....$13.00
WEAPONS..........$3.95	Prices for all of the above:	___Regular Edition
TOYS & MODELS...$3.95	___3rd Class.....$1.75	___Deluxe Edition
Prices for all of the above:	___1st Class.....$1.55	___U.S. Book rates
___3rd Class...$1.00 ea.	___Foreign Air...$2.50	............$2.00 ea.
___1st Class...$1.25 ea.	SPECIAL EFFECTS..$6.95	U.S. Priority.$2.57 reg.
___Foreign Air..$2.25 ea.	___3rd Class.....$1.50	............$3.30 deluxe
SPACESHIPS	___1st Class.....$2.00	Foreign Air..$7.00 reg.
(new enlarged)...$7.95	___Foreign Air...$5.50	............$8.50 deluxe
SPECIAL EFFECTS VOL. II		
..................$7.95	total enclosed: $_____	
TV EPISODE GUIDE BOOK	NYS residents add sales tax	
..................$7.95	Please allow 4 to 6 weeks for delivery of 3rd Class mail:	
ALIENS............$7.95	First Class delivery usually takes 2 to 3 weeks.	

ONLY U.S. Australia and New Zealand funds accepted.
Dealers: Inquire for wholesale rates on Photo Guidebooks.
NOTE: Don't want to cut coupon? Write order on separate piece of paper.

SEND TO: **TOWER BOOKS**
P.O. Box 511, Murry Hill Station
New York, N.Y. 10156

PLEASE SEND ME THE FOLLOWING TITLES:

Quantity	Book Number	Price

IN THE EVENT THAT WE ARE OUT OF STOCK ON ANY OF YOUR SELECTIONS, PLEASE LIST ALTERNATE TITLES BELOW:

Postage/Handling ☐

I enclose... ☐

FOR U.S. ORDERS, add 75¢ for the first book and 25¢ for each additional book to cover cost of postage and handling. Buy five or more copies and we will pay for shipping. Sorry, no C.O.D.'s.

FOR ORDERS SENT OUTSIDE THE U.S.A., add $1.00 for the first book and 50¢ for each additional book. PAY BY foreign draft or money order drawn on a U.S. bank, payable in U.S. ($) dollars.

☐ PLEASE SEND ME A FREE CATALOG.

NAME_____
(Please print)

ADDRESS_____

CITY_____ **STATE**_____ **ZIP**_____

Allow Four Weeks for Delivery